The Fabulous Flying Bicycle

Also by Glen Dines

The Mysterious Machine
Pitidoe the Color Maker
A Tiger in the Cherry Tree
The Useful Dragon of Sam Ling Toy

Library of Congress catalog card number: 60–5075

First Printing

The Macmillan Company, New York
Brett-Macmillan Ltd., Galt, Ontario
Printed in the United States of America

To my father
who likes to build things

CHAPTER 1

At the far end of his laboratory, G. Barnes, Scientist-Inventor, was all but hidden in a jungle of springs, wires, and metal rods. He glanced up and pushed his fingers through a thatch of brown hair. "Greetings, old buddy! This is your lucky day!"

Pudgy Bob Graham hesitated just inside the door. He looked about as happy as a snail crossing a freeway. "Ith it ready?" he lisped. "I got to deliver my paperth."

"Just a sec." G. (for Gerald) Barnes bent to tighten a bolt. "There! You are now the owner of a genuine G. Barnes Automatic Newspaper Launcher! Pretty slick, eh?"

"Well . . . I gueth tho. Doeth it work?"

The scientist-inventor adjusted his glasses, something

1

he did when he was thinking very hard. "I haven't exactly tested it, old buddy. . . ."

"Haven't tethted it! Holy cow, Jerry, what . . ."

Jerry waggled his hand. "Don't worry. That's what we're going to do now." He wrestled the cluttered bicycle through the door. "Did you bring your papers?"

"I left them in the alley. I didn't want . . . er . . . anything to happen."

"Just like everybody else in Saulito," Jerry muttered. "You'd think my lab was going to explode or something."

"Well," Bob giggled, "ath a matter of fact, it did! Jutht the other day!"

"Oh, that!" Jerry balanced the bike against the wall of his lab, which was actually a garage. "One little explosion . . ."

"Little! I heard it clear on the other thide of town! Boy, wath your father ever mad! Thay, where do I put the paperth?"

Jerry pointed to a narrow rack. "Right there. Then you wind the master spring, set this speed regulator and flip the release catch here. Understand?"

Bob shook his head.

"Here!" Jerry straddled the bike. "Hand me the papers. It works sort of like a crossbow, old buddy. That big spring in front is the bow. It shoots the papers out this tube." He stuffed the last newspaper into place and busied himself winding, setting and flipping. Then he pushed the bicycle into the alley. "Now, suppose you wanted to deliver a paper to that telephone pole."

Pudgy Bob giggled. "That'th thilly!"

"What?"

"Whoever heard of a telephone pole reading a newth-paper?"

"I didn't mean you were actually going to deliver a paper to a telephone pole. I meant . . . oh . . . never mind. Just pretend you are going to deliver a paper to that house." Jerry pointed toward the tiny, neat cottage of Miss Trimble, a tiny, neat and very fussy old maid. He pushed off. The top-heavy bike wobbled dangerously. Aiming quickly, he gritted his teeth and flipped the release catch.

"TWWWANNNG!" A tightly rolled newspaper shot out of the launching tube. By some miracle it missed the windows. However, a shower of shingles flew as the paper slammed into the roof, bounced thirty feet into the air and disappeared over the treetops in the next block.

"Holy cow!" Bob blurted.

The jolt of the launching had thrown Jerry flat. He clawed his way out from under newspapers, bicycle and a tangle of humming springs.

"Holy cow!" Bob repeated, crouching slightly as if he expected the newspaper to suddenly reappear.

Jerry struggled to his feet. "How about that?" he shouted, mustering as wide a grin as possible. "Right on target, eh, old buddy?"

"Holy cow!" Bob was beginning to sound like a broken record. "That paper wath going a thouthand mileth an hour!"

3

Jerry wrestled the bike upright, "I . . . ah . . . I had the master spring just a little too tight. But with some practice . . ."

Just then the back door of Miss Trimble's cottage flew open and Miss Trimble herself appeared. "What was that?" she shouted.

Jerry fumbled with his glasses. "Good morning, Miss Trimble. I'll be over this afternoon to fix . . . ah . . . to put back those shingles. You see, the master spring was a little too tight and so when I released the switch, the paper . . ."

Miss Trimble's face took on a look of sadness. "Please don't explain, Gerald. I wouldn't understand, anyway. I don't understand anything you do in that laboratory of yours. Just make sure you repair the damage."

"Oh, yes, ma'am," Jerry shouted, "first thing this afternoon."

The door of the cottage slammed.

"Goth, it'th lucky that paper didn't go through her window . . . or the wall or thomething like that! How'th my bike?"

"Not a scratch, old buddy!" Jerry patted his invention proudly. "Launcher's O.K., too. Just have to loosen this spring. There you go!" Jerry adjusted his glasses. "On second thought, maybe I'd better go with you. Sort of break it in."

"That'th fine with me. I'll get your bike."

Bob Graham's route covered the north end of Saulito. This had always puzzled Jerry since most of north Saulito was one steep hill. But now he saw that Bob's route in-

4

cluded the town's three bakery shops, two soda fountains and the one and only candy store. "Now I understand why Graham never loses weight." He glanced ahead. "Hey, Bob," he shouted, "you call out the addresses."

"O.K., Jerry. There'th the firtht one . . . that big brick houth on the corner."

Jerry shifted his weight to allow for the kick of the launcher, took careful aim and flipped the release. The newspaper soared gracefully over a nutmeg tree and plopped against the front door.

"Thay!" Bob squeaked in delight. "That wath real neat!"

Jerry was happy beyond words. He snapped off shot after shot. The launcher worked beautifully all the way up the hill.

They made the turn on Hillcrest and began to drop down into town. Jerry was so busy lining up a tricky, off-a-wall, left-hand spiral that he didn't notice the papers shift forward. He flipped the release. "TWWWANNNG!" The paper sizzled into space. The bike lurched and bounced against the curb. The shift had somehow managed to tighten the spring.

Bob ducked as the paper whistled past his ear. "Holy cow, Jerry! You thure missed . . . hey, wait a minute!" He stared as Jerry flashed by him. "Hey, thlow down! We turn at the nextht corner! Wait for me!"

Jerry twisted about. "Can't stop! Something's jammed in the chain!"

The hill was steep and getting steeper. To his horror, Jerry realized he was going too fast even to turn. In vain he clawed at the twanging spring lodged in the chain. The bike wobbled. He grabbed for the handle bar but clamped on the release catch instead. "Snap" something gave. With a clatter and twang the Barnes Automatic Newspaper Launcher began launching newspapers all by itself.

Spraying newspapers in every direction, Jerry swept into the center of town. "Thud!" "Slap!" "Clunk!" Tightly rolled newspapers bounced off fireplugs, walls and parking meters. One sailed through the open door of Tulles' barbershop and stuck, arrowlike, on a hatrack hook. Half a block farther, Mr. Giovanni, the grocer, bent forward to examine a cantaloupe which seemed suddenly to sprout the *Saulito Herald*.

Jerry twisted and skidded, sometimes guiding but mostly just managing to hang onto the bucking bike. Cars and trucks veered right and left. Shoppers scattered. A salvo of hissing papers crashed into the peaceful public square. People and pigeons scrambled in all directions.

A portly man came around the corner as Jerry swept by. He dodged one newspaper but a second plucked his cigar neatly from his lips. The woman behind him gasped at the sight of a cigar-smoking newspaper sailing through the air.

At the next corner an indignant citizen sprinted forward. "Hey, you!" he shouted. "Stop! You nearly hit me with that newspaper!" For a moment he looked like a TV western hero chasing after a runaway team. Then he was galloping in the opposite direction, followed closely by five fast-flying *Heralds*.

"I'm sorry, sir!" Jerry screeched. By now the bike had

6

slowed enough so that he could lurch in the direction of a less crowded side street. It was then that one of the front windows of Proctor's Hardware shivered and collapsed in a cascade of clinkling glass.

An instant later Jerry piled to a headlong halt into a mound of sawdust behind Stanley's Lumberyard. "Great spinning satellites!" he choked, fighting his way to the surface.

The sound of a siren pierced the air. He had the sudden urge to crawl back under as the black-and-white squad car, pride of Saulito's three-man police force, hove into view. The side door popped open and out bounced the huge police chief, his face creased with a look of anger and puzzlement.

Jerry shook sawdust from his hair and smiled widely. "Good morning, Police Chief Pinkerton, your honor, sir. Looks like summer is here, your honor, sir." Chief Pinkerton's "G. Barnes" frown called for the thickest layer of soft soap.

The huge man grunted, then grunted again. His face, pinkish by nature, was crimson. "BERALD GARNES!" he roared, ". . . I mean GERALD BARNES! WHAT HAVE YOU BEEN DOING NOW?"

Jerry adjusted his glasses. "Chief Pinkerton, sir, your honor . . ."

"NEVER MIND THAT 'YOUR HONOR' BA-LONEY! JUST ANSWER MY QUESTION!"

Jerry decided that a direct path might be the best. "Chief Pinkerton, sir, it worked fine when we went up the hill, but something got stuck in the chain as we came

8

down and the whole thing started to go like sixty. . . ."

"WHAT WHOLE THING?"

"The spring, sir."

"WHAT SPRING?"

"The master spring on my automatic newspaper launcher, sir."

Chief Pinkerton sighed heavily, "Where is it?"

Jerry pointed to the still-spinning wheel sticking out from the sawdust beside him.

The police chief glanced down. "That looks very much like a bicycle wheel to me."

"You're absolutely right, Chief Pinkerton, it is a bicycle wheel."

"Bicycle wheels don't throw newspapers through windows, Gerald."

"You're absolutely right, Chief Pinkerton. But this bicycle wheel happens to be part of the bicycle that my Barnes Automatic Newspaper Launcher is attached to. It's very simple. You pile the newspapers in the rack, wind the master spring . . ."

"Holy cow!" Bob Graham squealed, as he skidded to a stop. He let Jerry's bike tumble and began to paw furiously at the sawdust. "Goth thakes!" he sputtered angrily. "You and your crathy inventionth! Now I'll have to go back and pick up all thoth paperth and deliver them all over again!" The angry boy yanked his bike from the sawdust, tore the launcher loose and pedaled away. "From now on, Jerry Barnth," he shouted over his shoulder, "you can jutht keep your old inventionth to yourthelf!"

Chief Pinkerton nudged the crumpled launcher with

his toe, but pulled away quickly when the contraption gave a last twang. "Gerald," he began in a soft rumble, "I have often thought my job here in Saulito would be almost perfect if it weren't for YOU AND YOUR BLAMED INVENTIONS!"

"You're absolutely ri . . . I mean, I guess that's true, Chief Pinkerton, sir. But, honestly, I was just trying to help Bob. He works hard on his paper route. I thought this launcher would help him." ·

"That's all well and good, Jerry," observed Mr. Proctor, who had joined the chief, "but why do your inventions seem always to include my hardware store window? Last summer it was that confounded wire-controlled rocket you sent off, and before that some sort of flying saucer."

Jerry stood up and began brushing himself. "That is odd, isn't it? But I'll pay for the window. I worked all summer last year and I guess I'll just work all summer this year."

"Well," Chief Pinkerton shrugged, glancing warily at the launcher, "at least when you're working you can't invent. And when you can't invent, life is fairly peaceful in our little town. I guess I'll let it go at that."

"Thank you, Chief Pinkerton," Jerry murmured.

Mr. Proctor grunted. "Gerald, I have some storerooms you can clean up by way of paying for the window. Come in first thing tomorrow morning.

"Yes, sir." Jerry bent to pick up the launcher.

"OH, NO!" the police chief boomed. "I'll take that thing!"

10

Jerry shrugged as the portly policeman dragged his latest invention to the back of the squad car and stuffed it into the trunk.

Mr. Proctor turned as the chief drove away. "I'll see you tomorrow, Gerald . . . eight-thirty sharp!"

"Yes, sir, Mr. Proctor," Jerry nodded. Then he pulled his bike upright. "It's hard," he decided, "to be a scientist-inventor; especially in this town. But someday I'm going to have a laboratory all my own, maybe even underground, where I can experiment and invent to my heart's content." He giggled. "Underground lab! Imagine an underground scientific laboratory in Saulito. But then," he added, "if I really wanted a place to make secret inventions, an underground lab would be just the spot!"

CHAPTER 2

Afternoon brought with it the sultry threat of a summer thunderstorm. In company with three curious sparrows, Jerry perched atop Miss Trimble's roof fitting shingles back into place.

"Hey, spaceman!" Vic Lathrop was standing in the doorway of the lab.

"Over here!" Jerry waved. "Come on up!" He watched as Vic leaned his bike against the garage and easily cleared the four-foot fence bordering Miss Trimble's orderly yard. Although he and Vic were good friends, they were about as different as two people could be. Vic was tall and husky and kept his hair trimmed in a neat crew cut. He could outrun and outthrow everyone in their grade and most of the older kids in school.

Jerry giggled. As far as he was concerned, he dragged his bony frame into the barbershop only under protest. And, although he liked sports, he usually ended up deep in center field because of his habit of dreaming about amazing new inventions, when he should have been fielding easy grounders.

About the only thing he and Vic shared in common was the fun of doing things.

Vic scrambled up the ladder and boosted himself onto the roof. He eyed the scattered shingles. "Great little invention, spaceman! Porky Graham is sure mad at you. And did you see the cantaloupe Mr. Giovanni hung in his window?"

Jerry winced. He could even remember the sign that the jolly Italian grocer had lettered. "Believe it or don't!" the sign announced. "Newspaper growing out of cantaloupe or maybe other way round. LOOK!"

Vic picked up a shingle. "Guess you're lucky at that, though. Your launcher didn't do any real damage, except for Proctor's Hardware. Sure funny how your inventions always manage to end up on the wrong side of his windows."

"Mr. Proctor didn't think it was funny," Jerry sighed, as he fit the last shingle into place. He nailed it tight. "It's going to take at least two months' morning work to settle that score."

They both turned at the merry tinkling of the ice cream man's bell.

Jerry searched his empty pockets. "You have any loot?"

Vic shook his head.

"Oh, well," Jerry shrugged, "in this case just looking is a treat. Man oh man, get a load of those rear-vision mirrors!"

At least a dozen different mirrors fanned from both sides of the bicycle's fancy, blue-tinted windshield. The handle bar grips were made of bright red leather with long colored streamers at the tips. Three sets of glittering, chrome-plated rods connected the handle bars with the front wheel. And the wheel itself was all but covered with a cluster of generators, headlights, speedometers, sirens, clickers, reflectors, hand-brake cables and a complicated five-speed gear shift. The genuine sheepskin seat with red suede trim featured a jewel-studded tool pouch. The rear fender was complete with luggage rack, taillights, turning signals, whip aerials, framed license plates, ornamental figures and a giant red, white and blue mudguard.

The sun sparkled on the neat gold-leaf sign atop the colorful two-wheeled cart. "HAPPY TOM HAPPY'S ICE CREAM CART," Jerry read, his mouth watering, "27 assorted flavors." Then he snorted, "Happy Tom!" He glanced at the tall, lean proprietor of the mobile ice cream shop. "If that guy is happy, I'll eat my automatic newspaper launcher."

Happy Tom Happy's sad face never changed. He hardly ever talked, except for a curt "thank you." About the only thing that saved him from looking like a sad-faced robot was the twinkle in his dark eyes and a dangling lock of black hair.

Jerry eyed the solemn ice cream salesman a moment longer, then he turned. "Let's blast, muscles."

14

Vic scrambled down the ladder. Jerry followed. Half-way down, however, he stopped. Something seemed strange. He climbed back to the roof.

"What's the matter?" Vic questioned.

"I don't know exactly but there's something screwy. Come and look for yourself."

Together they watched as the man sped past, completely ignoring the flock of children that had scurried in answer to the bell.

Jerry shifted for a better look. "Doesn't it look like he's carrying something under his arm?"

"Yeah, but I can't see a thing."

"Something else, all-star. He's been rolling a block now, uphill, and he still hasn't pumped once!" Jerry adjusted his glasses. "Come on!" He clattered down the ladder, three rungs at a clip.

The next moment they both were astraddle their bikes and catapulting down the alley. A block ahead, the sad-faced salesman's bicycle was still moving steadily without benefit of legwork.

"Great sputtering nose cones!" Jerry muttered. "This is the craziest thing I've ever seen! He may have everything else on that bike, but he doesn't have a motor!"

"You can say that again! Let's follow!"

The salesman turned up Railroad Street, a little-used gravel road that skirted the Southern Pacific tracks. Keeping a safe distance, Jerry and Vic pedaled after.

Thunder rolled overhead as Happy Tom made a final turn and bounced along a dusty path which led to his house. More shack than anything else, the weathered little

15

clapboard building stood on a shrub-whiskered field, sheltered slightly by a thin stand of eucalyptus trees.

Both Jerry and Vic swerved behind a handy shield of brush. Jerry laid his bike on its side and peered through a gap in the thicket. He glanced up as the sun ducked behind a roll of gray clouds and thunder boomed again. "We're going to get soaked if we don't get under cover."

"Let's get under the trees," Vic whispered. He crouched low and circled into the eucalyptus grove. Jerry shadowed him, crunching carefully over the pungent carpet of bark and leaves.

The lanky man was busily unloading his cart. This seemingly finished, he bent over his bike and, as Jerry stared, went through the motions of lifting something from the luggage rack. Then, carefully cradling nothing at all, he stepped into the shack and closed the door behind him.

Jerry whistled. "Roaring red rockets! Either this character has a screw loose or we've stumbled onto the mystery of the year!"

Leaves rustled behind them. Jerry whirled, expecting to see an enraged ice cream salesman. Instead, a large raindrop splashed harmlessly in the loose undergrowth. More followed.

Suddenly a hissing came from inside the tiny shack. Jerry cocked his head. "That sounds like one of those big hydraulic carlifts in a service station!"

"Carlift!" Vic snorted. "There's hardly room in there for Happy Tom, let alone a carlift!"

The door of the shack popped open. The tall man re-

16

appeared and began pushing bike, cart and all toward the open door.

Jerry pressed forward. "Now, how is he going to get that whole thing into his shack? It's already filled with ice cr . . ." Suddenly he whipped off his glasses, rubbed them against his shirt, then jammed them back. It was still happening. "Vic, look! The luggage rack!" A misty spray of raindrop splashes formed the outline of something above the rack, where absolutely nothing appeared.

For one of the rare moments in his life, G. Barnes, Scientist-Inventor, was speechless. He stared, water streaming down his face, as Happy Tom, his bicycle and finally his ice cream cart slipped from sight. In the next minute hissing came once more from the weathered shack.

The sound helped bring Jerry out of his trance. He shook his head. "Sixty-six suffering sizzling satellites!" He glanced around.

Vic was already edging forward. "Come on, spaceman, I want a better look." Half creeping, half scurrying, they made their way to the corner of the shack. They crept along the wall. Vic was first at the window. With a quick jerk he glanced inside. "What . . ." he gasped.

"What what?" Jerry demanded.

"The shack! It's . . . it's *empty!*"

"Empty! You're crazy!" Jerry peered through the dusty, rain-streaked pane. "My gosh, you're right! It is empty . . . except for that bed and table!"

"Wouldn't that beat all!" Vic snorted in a loud voice. "Shhhhh!"

"Why shhhh? There's nobody in that shack, spaceman.

18

I don't know who's the craziest—we or that Happy Tom character." He began a comic imitation of the mysterious ice cream man carrying an invisible bundle.

Jerry might have joined in the fun but, for some reason, he stepped back and glanced above the window. Through a panel in the wall a huge eye fixed him in a steady, glassy stare. He gagged and pointed wildly. "A big eye . . . watching us! Let's get out of here!"

"THAT WOULD BE MOST UNWISE!"

Jerry jolted straight up. The voice had come from behind. He whirled to face a scowling Happy Tom Happy. His knees threatened to shake out from under him. "How . . . how do you . . . do?"

"At the moment," the tall man growled, choosing his words as carefully as a surgeon selects his sharpest knives, "I am more interested in what *you* are doing."

"Well, sir . . . er . . . I was . . . that is . . . we were . . ."

"Snooping," the lanky man muttered.

"Snooping?" Jerry echoed.

"Snooping."

Jerry hadn't thought of it in quite that way, but that is what they had been doing. Embarrassment burned on his cheeks. "You're right, Mr. . . . er . . . Mr. Happy. We were snooping. I'm sorry."

Vic broke in. "We aren't going to do any . . . harm."

The tall man nodded.

Jerry, now in full control of his knees, studied him. There was something about this lanky, black-haired man

20

that seemed familiar. Then he remembered a picture in his history book. Happy Tom looked exactly like a young Abraham Lincoln. Even his expression was the same. Sad and wise, Jerry thought. He turned and stared up at the huge glass "eye." "Maybe it's a kind of spyglass, or even . . ."

" . . . television," Happy Tom announced, as if he had been reading his mind.

Jerry twirled about. "Huh?"

"Television," the lanky man repeated. "You parked your bikes behind that bush, which I planted there for good reason, circled into the eucalyptus and peeked into the window."

"You mean you have this sha . . . I mean your home here, rigged with television? You were watching all the time?"

Once again Happy Tom nodded.

Jerry fumbled with his glasses. It was now plain that Mr. Happy Tom Happy was something more than a sad ice cream salesman who looked like Abraham Lincoln.

"Of course," Happy Tom murmured, "you realize I could have stopped you when you were crouching behind that bush?"

Jerry nodded. He hadn't realized this at all, but it seemed a good idea to agree. A quick look told him that Vic was also in an agreeing mood.

"Usually I discourage trespassers before they even get that far."

Jerry was happy that the lanky man didn't use the word

"snooper." Then he realized that Happy Tom was through talking altogether. The tall man had walked past them and was turning the corner.

"What'll we do now?" Vic whispered.

"We can either clear out or follow him, I guess."

"Well?"

"I'm for following him."

"Check."

Together they scampered around the corner and crowded through the doorway.

Jerry stood for a moment, letting his eyes adjust to the darkness. The room was hot and heavy with the musty stench of old wood and yellow-stained paper. The sound of his scuffling feet echoed strangely loud. In the far corner he could make out a squatty table with a dusty, torn oil-cloth draped over it. Near the opposite wall, at the foot of the rusty metal bed, stood Happy Tom.

Jerry searched the walls. Above each window was a tiny box. "If those are television cameras," he said to himself, "they're certainly the smallest in the world. But still, old 'Honest Abe' here knows everything we did!"

He eyed the tall, silent man. A question danced just out of reach. Something Happy Tom had said . . . or hadn't said. A sudden shiver tingled up his spine as the question formed in his mind. "Why hadn't Mr. Happy stopped Vic and me," Jerry asked himself, "if he knew we were hiding behind the bush watching him?" Jerry stared. "Unless," he added silently, "unless this strange guy wanted us . . . wanted us . . ." His lips formed the words he couldn't speak.

22

"Unless I wanted to get you into the shack?" The gloomy man's question hung in the air like a poised hawk.

"Huh?" Vic blurted. "What do you mean?"

The tall man turned abruptly and began chanting numbers into empty air. "Seven . . . nine . . . three . . . four." The door slammed shut.

"Locked!" Vic gasped. "Jerry, the door is locked . . ."

His words were drowned under a great hissing, louder than before.

"Oh, my gosh!" Jerry shrieked, as the floor of the tiny shack began to tremble. He felt himself going down, down, down.

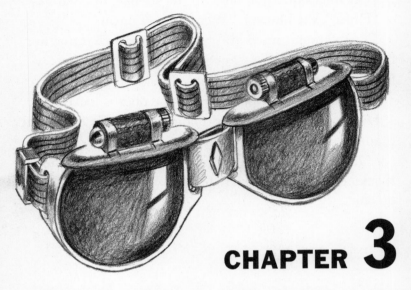

CHAPTER 3

The floor quivered underfoot. The awful hissing crushed against Jerry's ears. The windows of the shack shrank to tiny squares of sunlight before the floor came to rest with a clunk. Jerry lurched forward and thrust out his arm for support. His hand pressed against a cool metal wall. They were at the bottom of a deep shaft.

Once more Happy Tom began to chant, "Three . . . six . . . nineteen."

Jerry heard a muffled click. He whirled. A section of the wall slid silently to one side, revealing a huge room bathed in an eerie blue-green glow.

Mr. Happy strode forward. "Wait here!" he ordered, as he stepped across a red line painted on the floor. He paused, extended his arms, took a few skittering sidesteps

24

and then began to make his way the length of the huge vault. But instead of walking straight, he did a little dance, moving right, then left, a few steps forward, then right again.

"What in the world?" Jerry snorted.

"That guy sure likes to make it hard for himself," Vic whispered.

"You said it, all-star!" Jerry stepped from the shaft and cautiously toed the red line. "But then, after that elevator ride, nothing would surprise me!"

By now Mr. Happy's weird dance had taken him half the length of the room.

"I'd sure like to know what he's doing," Vic puzzled. "Why all this zigzag business?"

Jerry shrugged. "At least we found out about the hissing." He glanced about, only to discover that the wall had slid back into place. "Oh, my gosh, Vic, look! The wall . . ."

Vic turned. "Good grief, every time we walk through something it shuts tight behind us. What's going on here?"

Jerry faced about. "There's one way to find out. Oh, no! Now 'Honest Abe' is gone!" The tall ice cream salesman had seemingly vanished into the wall at the far end of the huge room. "This is too much! Let's go see . . ." Jerry took a step forward then staggered back. "Hey, Vic," he gasped, "what hit me?"

"Huh?" Vic blurted. "Hit you?"

Jerry felt the painful knot swelling on his forehead. "Yes, something hard . . . hit me right on the forehead!"

25

"What's the matter with you, Jerry? There's nothing . . . ouch!" Now it was Vic's turn to stagger. "My gosh, there is something!" He was staring into emptiness. "It's as hard as cement!"

Jerry raised his arms and took a cautious step. Something hard whacked against his shin. "Ow! My leg! My leg!" He hopped about on one leg, massaging his throbbing shin. Something else caught him in the rear. With a "whuff" he pitched face first. "Don't move, Vic, we're surrounded!"

Vic advanced to the red line and crouched in a boxer's pose; his right hand cocked, his left extended. He pawed cautiously, then began busily exploring the air in front of him. "My gosh," Vic scurried back and forth along the line, patting with both bands, "there's something here! My gosh! It's a wall!"

Jerry pushed himself up and hobbled to Vic's side. He saw nothing, but his outstretched fingers pressed against solidness. He ran his hand along the smooth surface.

A panel suddenly shot back in the far wall of the huge room, revealing the lanky outline of Happy Tom. The man repeated his strange dance, but this time he moved much more rapidly. Jerry squinted into the curtain of blue-green light. Mr. Happy was wearing some sort of goggles. A few more zigs and zags and the tall man stepped over the red line. He held out two pairs of goggles identical to his. "Put these on."

Jerry examined his. The lenses were made of thick green glass, embedded with a network of fine silver wires. They reminded him of the safety goggles machinists wear.

Slipping them over his own glasses, he straightened and blinked. The huge room wasn't empty at all. It was filled with shimmering, glasslike blocks stacked five and six high, wall to wall. Jerry ran his hands over the sides of the piled cubes. They looked like glass but didn't have the brittle feel of glass. They felt more like polished plastic.

Vic was busy hefting one of the cubes. "No wonder you raised a knot on your head! These things are heavy! What are they?"

"Transoplastic," Mr. Happy announced.

"Transo what?"

"Transoplastic."

"Transo . . . plastic," Jerry repeated, adjusting his goggles. "Transo . . ."

"Invisible," the tall man explained, "except when you're using Visiospecs." He touched his goggles.

"And hard!" Jerry added, feeling his forehead. He looked over the huge room. "Did you . . ."

". . . make all these?" the tall man completed his question. "Yes, I'm a scientist. As a matter of fact, I'm a genius."

"A genius?" Jerry breathed. This was the first time he'd ever heard anyone call himself a genius with a straight face. And Mr. Happy's was as straight a face as he'd ever seen. Something about the way the man said it, however, made it sound like a simple statement of fact.

"This is my storage vault," Mr. Happy continued. "Come along, I'll show you the lab."

Jerry followed Mr. Happy into a narrow, zigzag passageway through the transoplastic. "You could get lost in

28

here," he giggled. "Without Visiospecs you could never make it through."

"Or out again," Vic added in a whisper.

Jerry stopped laughing.

At the far wall Mr. Happy began another chant. "Nine . . . twenty-one . . . thirteen." A section of the wall rolled aside. "Step through," he directed. "Take off your Visiospecs."

Jerry stepped forward, pulling off the heavy goggles. He squinted in the sudden brightness. The room was smaller than the storage vault. "My gosh!" he gasped, as his eyes focused on a vast array of flasks, bottles, tubes, pipes, gauges and instruments all burbling and bubbling and burping and making little humming noises.

The walls were lined with sinks, shelves and work-benches. In the far corner, above a switch-studded control panel, a giant television screen stretched nearly five feet across the wall. When Mr. Happy twisted a knob, a section of the screen suddenly enlarged. Jerry could actually make out ants crawling up a tree trunk. "Look at that! No wonder he knew what we were doing!"

"Huh?" Vic grunted.

"Don't you recognize those trees and that bush? Look, you can even see our bikes!"

"Man oh man, it's a complete view around the sha . . . I mean Mr. Happy's house!"

"Shack is right, Vic," the tall man corrected. "Actually, I live in here."

Jerry surveyed a comfortable apartment which opened off the lab. The floors were covered with deep rugs. Be-

29

tween well-filled bookcases and beautiful pictures, the walls glowed with some kind of built-in lighting.

Vic's voice came from the lab. "Hey, spaceman, look what I found!" He was standing beside Happy Tom Happy's combination bicycle and ice cream cart.

"This is the greatest!" Jerry bubbled. He faced the tall man. "Did you build all this yourself?"

Mr. Happy nodded. "Of course, I designed some special equipment to do the digging."

"You must work real fast." Vic's words were edged with disbelief. "You haven't been in Saulito very long. I can remember when you first started selling ice cream."

"So can I," Jerry added. "It was just last summer when those motorcycle guys . . . a . . ."

"The Black Angels," Vic interrupted.

"Yes, when the Black Angels were causing so much trouble in town, racing around and crazy things like that."

"Didn't they sort of pick on you?" Vic questioned.

The tall man nodded. "Still do."

"Aw, they're just a bunch of screwballs!" Jerry snorted. "But this lab is the greatest! All this equipment and that big TV and the storage room out there. I'll bet it's bigger than the high school gym!"

"And sliding doors and hidden passageways," Vic added grimly.

"You're both probably wondering why I am showing you all my secrets," Mr. Happy murmured.

"You're absolutely right," Jerry grinned. Mr. Happy was now answering questions he hadn't even thought of.

30

The tall man sat on the edge of a metal-topped work-bench. "It's quite simple. I need your help."

"What?" Vic narrowed his eyes. "*You* need *our* help?"

Happy Tom Happy pushed a dangling lock of hair from his forehead. "As you can see, I have perfected a colorless, rustproof, extra-strong, completely transparent plastic which can be used in many important ways. However, T-36—that's its scientific name—will simply go to waste unless people, many people, learn about it."

Jerry was very busy adjusting his glasses. "You want us to . . ."

". . . help present transoplastic in a dramatic way, so that in the shortest time as many people as possible will learn about it," Mr. Happy finished.

Jerry slumped. All this keen equipment, he thought, a real, honest-to-goodness underground lab almost in the middle of Saulito, and all he wants us to do is present this T-36 stuff to a whole bunch of people.

The tall scientist seemed to sense his disappointment. "Jerry," he murmured, "so far you and Vic are the only people in the entire world who know my secret. It's no accident that I chose you. For as long as I have been in Saulito I have watched your scientific progress."

Jerry straightened slightly.

"And, Vic, I know about your being president of your class, an outstanding athlete—and probably one of the most popular boys in town. And, being Jerry's best friend, you'll have to admit that his inventions attract public attention if, unfortunately, nothing else."

Even Jerry chuckled.

"So, you see, I'm asking you two because I know you can help me . . . and keep my secret at the same time."

"You mean you had this planned all the time?" Vic blurted. "You've been watching us and planned this whole thing?"

Mr. Happy nodded.

Jerry thumped his forehead. "Then you saw us up on Miss Trimble's roof!"

"Yes."

Jerry grinned. "There we were playing the big detectives and all the while you had planned the whole thing." He glanced toward the ice cream cart. "I still don't understand . . ."

"The bicycle is powered by a solar-electric motor," Mr. Happy broke in, skipping ahead to Jerry's next question. "Several of those rear-vision mirrors are actually sun reflectors. They gather in the sun's heat and convert it into electrical power." Happy Tom touched a button on the side of the colorful cart. A hidden door slid open. Behind it was a maze of wires and connections. "A simple little gadget," he added, without sounding boastful. "One of the things I've built to help pay my way while I've been working on the transoplastic." He straightened. "This is an aerial for a remote control, radio-recording alarm system, which I have here in the lab. Listen." Stepping to a control panel, he flipped a switch. From somewhere in the lab came the sound of scurrying footsteps.

"Wouldn't that beat all!" a familiar voice announced.

Jerry giggled.

"Why 'shhhh'?" someone answered.

"There's nobody in that shack, spaceman," the first voice continued.

"Hey," Vic burst out, "that's me!"

Vic's voice continued from a hidden loud-speaker. ". . . who's the craziest, we or that Happy Tom character." The voice faded.

"Man oh man," Vic muttered, "we didn't have a chance. The only thing you don't have is a picture of us peeking in the window . . . oh, no!"

Mr. Happy slid back the top of a small box fastened to the wall and handed Vic a slightly damp but very clear photograph.

Jerry peered over his friend's shoulder. "Look at that expression on your face, all-star."

"How about yourself, lionheart. You look like a kitten in a dog kennel!"

"I think you'll agree there's little chance of anyone discovering the secret of my transoplastic," Mr. Happy murmured. "Its first public presentation will be a surprise. Now, I need you two to make it colorful and dramatic. I hope you will help me, but I want you to take your time in deciding."

Jerry glanced about. As far as he was concerned, he was ready to start then and there.

Vic, however, shifted nervously. "O.K., Mr. Happy," he muttered. "Hey, speaking of time, it's almost six. We'd better head for home, Jerry."

33

Jerry nodded. He slipped on the green-lensed Visio-specs and followed as Mr. Happy led the way through the stacks of glowing blocks.

Not until they stepped through the doorway of the shack did the sad-faced man speak. "I hope to see you and Vic again," he whispered, as Vic ran on ahead. "We scientists have to stick together, you know."

Jerry seemed to be floating on a cloud of pride and happiness. "A real, live honest-to-goodness scientific genius," he murmured, "with a real honest-to-goodness underground laboratory. And he wants me to help him. Great gravitating gismos!"

Vic glanced around. "What did you say?"

"Oh, nothing, all-star. I was just thinking about poor, old, sad Happy Tom Happy working his fingers to the bone; slaving so that the world can enjoy the amazing transoplastic. Remember how those Black Angels gave him all that trouble? But Happy Tom Happy—brave, sad, poor, defenseless . . ."

"Nuts!" Vic snapped, dodging a rut in the road. "Defenseless, my foot! He's got more gadgets guarding that crazy shack than a whole atomic bomb factory—television, radio recorders, cameras, sliding doors, all kinds of electrical gismos! Why, an ant couldn't sneak into that lab! Not only that, but he admitted he had been spying on us for a year!"

Jerry felt himself slipping off his cloud of happiness.

"And, in case you've forgotten, those loudmouthed Black Angels gave him a bad time until about three of them showed up with bandages all over their heads.

Happy Tom Happy is about as defenseless as the United States Marine Corps!"

Jerry was slipping fast now. He tried to pull himself back onto his rosy cloud. "Are you telling me that Happy Tom beat up three Black Angels all by himself?"

"I'm not trying to tell you anything, spaceman, but it's awfully funny that three guys who had been giving 'poor, old, defenseless' Happy Tom a rough time should suddenly have the same kind of accident at the same time!"

Jerry stared at the road ahead. His happiness cloud melted from sight. "Vic's right," he told himself, although he hated to admit it. "Well," he added aloud, "if old 'Honest Abe' is trying to hide something, he sure chose a funny way to do it. He not only showed us the transo-plastic, but his lab and that keen little apartment—and told us about the TV and the radio recorder . . ."

"Just the same, spaceman, we'd better watch our step. I'll bet he hasn't shown us half his tricks!"

Jerry glanced at Vic. "I'm all for helping him, anyway. Sounds like a lot of fun. How about you?"

Vic shrugged. "Sure, but we'd better watch our step. We might end up looking from the inside out of one of those transo-whatchamacallit blocks!"

"Now, there's a pleasant thought," Jerry muttered.

CHAPTER 4

His morning chores at Proctor's Hardware completed, G. Barnes, Scientist-Inventor, bent over his cluttered workbench. The job at the hardware store was better than he expected. Not only was he replacing the broken window at about three square inches per day, but he had first choice of all the castoff screws, bolts, pipes and other odds and ends.

One such bolt flipped from his fingers and hid itself somewhere in the jumble beneath his bench.

"Darn!" Jerry snorted, as he pawed about on hands and knees. "Maybe I should work in Happy Tom's lab." He imagined himself busy among all the shiny, clicking instruments. Then he pictured a wrench slipping from his hand and smashing one of the shiny, clicking and very expensive instruments. "Anyway," he decided, rescuing the bolt from beneath an old motorcycle generator, "I want to surprise Vic and Happy Tom."

Straightening, he fitted the bolt into place and cocked his head to survey his handiwork.

The sound of a bike rattling in the alley was followed by a shower of gravel against the side of the garage and the metallic snap of a kickstand. Jerry grinned. Vic was the only guy in town who could turn a corner, skid to a stop, hop off his bike and stamp down his kickstand all in one easy motion.

Vic burst through the door. "Drop your gun, scarface! The place is surrounded!"

"No you don't! One more step and I'll blow this garage to smithereens!"

"Will Scarface Barnes blow the garage to smithereens? Will . . . oh, no!" Vic stared at Jerry's latest brainstorm.

Jerry shrugged. Vic's "what now" expression, closely akin to Chief Pinkerton's "G. Barnes" frown, was not new to him. "It's done, all-star—the Barnes Wire-controlled Satellite. Did you bring the snaps?"

Vic's eyes narrowed. "Wire-controlled satellite? I thought you were working on something that would . . ." he glanced over his shoulder ". . . help Mr. Happy present his transo-whatchamacallit!"

"Transoplastic," Jerry corrected, then he gestured toward the workbench. "This is it, all-star . . . the greatest!" He took the paper sack from Vic's hands. "Thanks for getting the snaps."

"Why don't you just invent things that stay in one

37

spot?" Vic asked, in a tone usually reserved for puppies and children.

Jerry was busy with the snaps. "You sound just like my dad, old pal. It might interest you to know that this latest Barnes invention will stay in one spot—at least part of it."

"Yeah," Vic nodded, "but it's that other part that usually ends up on the wrong side of Mr. Proctor's window!"

"Wait until you see this masterpiece in action. You'll be sorry you made fun of your poor, old, hard-working buddy."

"I'll bet!"

"Here," Jerry thrust out a spool of lightweight cable, "take this." He turned and picked up the two halves of the hollow metal ball Vic had been staring at. "I've already set up my launching pole."

Vic nearly dropped the spool. "Launching! Did you say launching?"

"Don't worry, just follow me. I'll bet umpteen million dollars you can't guess where we are going."

Vic eyed the metal ball. "To the hospital?"

"Very funny, I'm sure!" Jerry sniffed. "As a matter of fact, we are going to pay a visit to our good friend, Police Chief Pinkerton."

"Huh?" The spool of cable bounced on the floor. "You know what? I thought you said we were going to visit Chief Pinkerton! Isn't that a riot?"

Jerry straddled his battered bike. "Nothing funny about it. I'm going to ask Chief Pinkerton if I can test my satellite—and quit dropping that cable!"

"You what?" Vic gasped. "You . . . you're going to *ask* Chief Pinkerton?"

Jerry waved his hand impatiently. "This is a business matter, muscles. We want to tell a lot of people about something in a very short time, right? Unfortunately," he continued, as he pedaled into the alley, "sooner or later this will involve our old buddy, Chief Pinkerton. I've decided to make it sooner."

"I wonder what Chief Pinkerton is going to decide?"

For once Vic was content to follow as Jerry lead the way toward the two-story brick police station. Jerry stopped in front and leaned his bike very carefully against the wall. Then he paused to admire the black-and-white squad car, pride of Saulito's three-man police force. "They sure keep it shiny, don't they, inside and out!"

"Uh-huh," Vic chortled, "and that's where Chief Pinkerton is—inside the station!"

"O.K.! O.K.!" Jerry took a deep breath and pushed open the door. The air was heavy with the piny smell of disinfectant. The only sound was the whisk-whisking of a big overhead fan. The huge police chief was busy at his desk.

"Ahem," Jerry coughed. "Pardon me, sir, your honor."

When the big man pivoted, the bearings of his chair squealed in protest. His face wrinkled into the "G. Barnes" frown. "WELL?" he boomed.

Jerry retreated a step. "Sir," he thrust out the two halves of the satellite, "guess what I'm holding!"

Chief Pinkerton sat upright. His eyes darted from half to half, but he seemed most fascinated with the quivering

antennas. Suddenly his phone jangled. He shot out of his chair. "TURN 'EM OFF!"

"What?"

"THOSE . . . THEM . . . THEY . . . RINGING! TURN THEM OFF!"

Jerry looked at his dismembered satellite. "Oh, no, sir, your honor, these aren't making a sound. See?" He pushed toward the big policeman.

"WOFT!" Chief Pinkerton brushed aside a quivering antenna. "Oh, yes, the telephone! Get that thing out of my face!" He snatched up the jangling phone. "Saulito Police Department . . . Gerald Bombs . . . I mean, Chief Pinkerton speaking."

40

"It happens every time," Jerry whispered. "Sometimes I think Chief Pinkerton doesn't trust me!"

Vic snickered. "Why, Gerald Bombs, wherever did you get that idea?"

Chief Pinkerton finished his phone conversation and eased back into his chair. "Now, Gerald," he began in a strained whisper, "without shoving that whatever-it-is into my face or trying to interest me in question-and-answer games, just tell me WHAT DO YOU WANT?"

Jerry winced. "I'm sorry, your honor, if I startled you."

"The mere mention of your name startles me. Now, what is it?"

"Well, sir, your honor, I'm here on a matter of business. I want to test my double-safe, nonexploding, absolutely harmless, wire-controlled satellite . . ."

"Hold it!" The man waved his hand. "Satellite?"

"Satellite."

"Isn't that something that WHIRLS AROUND IN SPACE?"

"Well, yes."

"NO!" The chief turned back to his work.

"No what?"

"No, you can't test your double-exploding, nonwired, harm-controlled satellite!"

"But Chief Pinkerton, sir, your honor, my satellite won't whirl around in space. It will just whirl around a pole."

"Will it move?"

"Yes."

"NO!"

"Chief Pinkerton, sir, your honor, this is by far the

41

safest invention I've ever invented. I've already set up a launching pole in the middle of that big vacant field near the high school . . ."

"LAUNCHING POLE!"

"It's really a clothesline pole with a sort of cap on the top—very simple." Jerry stepped forward. "Let me show you. Now, these two halves go together like this. Er . . . that is . . . funny, they went together before . . ."

"Gerald," the big policeman murmured, "Gerald . . . GERALD! You have my tie caught in your satellite!"

"Oh, my gosh! Sort of tore it, didn't I? I'm sorry."

"So am I."

"But, anyway, the satellite fits together like this. Vic has the wire cable that will hold it to the launching pole . . . very strong cable. And that's all."

"There's just one other thing. How do you plan to make your satellite move . . . whirl . . . spin?"

"Oh, yes, right here and here I will attach two . . . er . . . harmless, nonexploding . . . kind of . . . er . . . rockets."

"NO!"

"No? But, sir, your honor, this is important. I'm not doing this just for myself . . ." Jerry swallowed his words. "I mean . . . er . . . I'm doing this for . . . society."

"Society!" the police chief snorted. "Your inventions are a menace to society!"

"But, Chief Pinkerton, this is perfectly harmless. All it will do is spin around a pole in the middle of a big vacant lot. And if anything happens, I promise I'll throw the whole thing away!"

42

Chief Pinkerton leaned back in his chair. He tapped his finger tips together. "I'm sure there are many vacant lots in China or Siberia . . ."

Vic broke in on the chief's heavy-handed humor. "Honestly, Chief Pinkerton, this is important. And it's the first time I can remember Jerry asking your permission to test one of his inventions. That should be worth something."

The big policeman rubbed his neck. "You have a point there."

Jerry broke in. "You certainly must know something about machinery to keep your squad car so shiny and nice. Why don't you come with us, sir, just to make sure everything goes all right."

"This is a switch," Chief Pinkerton chortled. "All right. But remember, if I don't like one little part of what I see, the whole thing is off!"

"Yes, sir!"

The big policeman stepped to a doorway. "Woods," he shouted, "watch the front. I'll be back in an hour or so."

When they reached the vacant lot Jerry and Vic climbed out of the gleaming squad car and raced toward a pole standing in the center. The huge policeman ambled behind, followed by a yammering herd of small boys attracted by the sight of the squad car.

"Hey, Jerry," one of them shouted, "whatcha going to do?"

"What's the pole for?" another squealed.

Jerry ignored their questions. He directed Vic to unroll the cable. Then he knelt to attach the cable end and two

43

tiny rocket units to the shiny, antenna-sprouting ball. He fed the cable through a pulley, then snapped the whole thing to a ring that encircled the pole.

"See, your honor, sir?" He pointed. "It's designed so that if anything goes wrong, all you have to do is hold onto the end of this cable and the satellite will wrap itself . . ."

"Just a minute!" Chief Pinkerton snorted. "Would you repeat that?"

"Certainly, your honor. I said that the satellite will wrap itself around the pole . . ."

"No, no! Who did you say was going to hold the cable?"

"Well, sir, your honor, Vic and I will be very busy firing those rockets."

The policeman rubbed his neck. He walked to the end of the cable. "It looks all right so far," he shouted. "I guess maybe it will work."

"Here, Vic," Jerry directed, "take this match. When I give the word, light the rocket. Are you ready, Chief?"

The big man picked up the cable and gave it a little tug. He nodded.

Jerry knelt beside Vic. "I haven't had a chance to tell you how this thing works, have I?"

"If it works!"

"Very funny. It's simple. We light these rockets and 'whoosh'—the satellite goes around and around."

"Yes, siree, that's real simple! But how is it going to help old Happy Tom?"

Jerry glanced up to see the tall scientist watching from the far edge of the field. "My gosh, there he is!"

44

"Who?"

"Old Happy Tom himself! All the better. Now, look, Vic, when we're ready to present the transoplastic we'll build a launching tower about a hundred feet high. We'll have fifty umpteen satellites spinning around it," Jerry spread his arms, "and each one will be towing a big, long sign like SEE THE AMAZING TRANSOPLASTIC or BUY TRANSOPLASTIC NOW or GET YOUR KICKS FROM T-36! Got your match ready?"

"Get your kicks from T-36? Oh, no! What's this thing?" Vic stared at the metal ball.

"An air whistle. Each satellite will come equipped with a different kind of noisemaker. Man oh man, all-star, I can hardly wait! Let's get this thing into orbit!" Jerry struck his match. "Ready for the blast-off?"

Both rockets sizzled to life. Jerry gave the satellite a little toss. It dipped, straightened, then soared away in a flat arc, whistling beautifully.

Vic sprinted to a safe distance. Jerry, however, stood admiring his latest brainstorm. He took a few backward steps and tripped over the cable. The screaming satellite swished over his head, much too close for comfort.

"Come on, Jerry," Vic called, "get out of there!"

Still watching the circling ball, Jerry scrambled to his feet and took another step. He tumbled once again. His leg was caught in the cable. He wiggled. The cable held fast. The satellite was flashing toward him again. He panicked and kicked. The cable dropped away from his leg and, at the same time, jerked free from a surprised Chief Pinkerton.

The satellite swerved outward. The loose cable slithered over the ground, writhing and lashing like an angry snake. Then it snarled in the pulley. Both ball and cable came slashing toward Jerry, neck high! He twirled and dived headlong. The cable whistled murderously overhead.

Hugging the base of the wobbling pole, Jerry peeked over his shoulder. Just beyond the arc of the rocketing satellite stood Vic. Beyond him, surrounded by a gang of jumping, gesturing kids, was Chief Pinkerton. Mr. Happy had disappeared. "Just as well. If I could only get that cable unsnarled. Oh, my gosh!" The ring had stopped turning. The snarled cable was busily wrapping itself down the pole!

Jerry slithered about. "Vic," he screamed, "Chief Pinkerton! The cable—it's wrapping around the pole!"

Both Vic and the chief returned his frantic shouts with cheerful waves.

"No! NO!" Jerry pointed as best he could. "The cable —it's caught! It's twisting around the pole!"

This time Vic clasped his hands over his head in the boxer's victory sign.

Jerry groaned. The scream of the satellite and the yammering kids were drowning out his voice. Overhead, the cable was flapping "whoppity-whop" lower and lower. "I can't even crawl out now! I'd get about halfway and 'wham-o' the cable would slice me like a piece of baloney!" He cupped his hands around his mouth. "VIC, VIC, CABLE'S WRAPPING . . . ON POLE!"

A sudden look of alarm spread over Vic's face. He

tugged at the policeman's sleeve, shouting and pointing. Chief Pinkerton did a funny little dance, then lumbered toward his squad car.

Jerry fumbled for his glasses, but he was pressing so hard against the ground he couldn't reach them. He thought of grabbing the cable, but then what would he do about the satellite?

"Whoppity-whoppity-whop," the cable wound faster and faster as the satellite's round trips grew shorter and shorter.

Then Jerry heard the wail of a siren. He raised his head an inch to see the bright red Saulito fire truck bounce onto the field in a great cloud of dust. Jerry thought he saw

the lanky figure of Happy Tom close beside the white-helmeted fire captain.

Several firemen came running forward, dragging a hose between them. A jet of water erupted from the nozzle. Water and satellite met with a "whoosh." The metal ball slowed, then bounced on the ground. The firemen moved in, skillfully directing the jet of water until it pinned the bucking satellite to earth. A geyser of mud gushed into the air.

"NOW!" Chief Pinkerton roared.

Jerry scrambled to his feet and slipped and slid his way across the mud.

The firemen jerked their water stream away and the satellite bounced and spun until it wrapped itself tightly against the pole.

Jerry took a deep breath. "Great sputtering spaceships! That was . . . real . . . close . . ." The look on Vic's face made him stop. He turned. Chief Pinkerton was standing by his shiny black-and-white squad car. Only it wasn't shiny or black and white. It was an ugly, mud-spattered brown. One side of the chief's face was also brown. The other side was deep red.

Jerry mustered up a broad grin. "Well, sir, your honor, I guess I'll just throw it away. Like you said . . . throw it away."

The big policeman dug mud from his ear. "Yes," he rumbled, "by all means throw it away—the pole, the cable, the big, shiny ball, the rockets—especially the rockets."

48

"Thank you very much, sir, your honor. You saved my life. That was real fast thinking. And thank you, sir," Jerry turned to the fire captain, "and your firemen. I'm sorry about the squad car, Chief Pinkerton, I really am. And I'm sorry about . . . er . . . the mud and I'm sorry . . ."

"Throw it all into a big hole," Chief Pinkerton continued, "and cover it up. And then, Gerald, one thing more."

Jerry smiled brightly. "Yes, sir, your honor?"

"If I catch you inventing anything else that moves, spins, shakes, ROLLS, BOUNCES, QUIVERS OR EVEN TREMBLES, I'M GOING TO THROW *YOU* IN A HOLE!"

"Yes, sir, your honor."

Jerry's answer was followed by a chorus of hoots from the small-fry onlookers. He ignored them until Red Davis, a tall, bony boy, took up the chant. "That's a real crazy invention, except it doesn't work; just like all your other crazy ideas!" The redhead bent double guffawing at his own joke.

Jerry gritted his teeth. "Don't kill yourself laughing, Red."

Red continued playing to his audience of jeering small fry. "Real crazy invention is right, you silly jerk!"

"Who are you calling a jerk?"

Red swallowed and stared. "I'm calling you a jerk, jerk!" His mouth curled in a tight smile. "You're always coming up with these crazy stunts, four-eyes!"

Despite the fact that Red was heavier and a good head

50

taller, Jerry took a step forward. "You'd better watch who you call a jerk!" he growled.

Red swung off his bike. "Yeah? Whatch goin' do about it, skinny?"

"You'd better shut your mouth," Vic cut in, "or I'm going to shut it for you!"

Red's smirk changed to a pout. "I . . . I was talking to four-eyes, here. What business you got . . ."

"I'm making it my business."

Red straightened his bike. "O.K., O.K., but you just wait, Jerry jerk. I'll catch you alone sometime!"

Jerry snatched off his glasses and handed them to Vic. "All right, big mouth, there's no time like the present!"

Red squinted. "Real brave, aren't you? As long as Vic is around . . ."

Jerry lunged forward and sent the taller boy's bike crashing to one side. "This is just between you and me," he snarled, anger throbbing in his clenched fists. "Come on, big mouth, if you're going to do something, do it now!"

Red's mouth dropped open. It was plain to even the smallest of the crowd that he had dried up and was about ready to blow away.

It was then that Chief Pinkerton stepped between them. "All right, all right, one mix-up a day is enough!"

Slipping on his glasses, Jerry stood for a moment letting the heat drain from his chest. Red scuttled after his bike and wheeled away.

"What a deal," Jerry muttered, as he scooped up a badly battered satellite.

The trip back to the police station was not a happy one.

Chief Pinkerton was about as friendly as a boil. Vic was lost somewhere behind a thoughtful frown. He nodded absently when Jerry suggested washing the mud-covered squad car.

"How can we attract attention with something that doesn't move?" Jerry quizzed, as he applied the finishing touches to the once more shiny squad car. "Oh, well, we scientists must suffer. Hey, speaking of suffering, that's just what I was doing until the chief thought of calling the fire department."

Vic straightened from wringing washrags. "It was Happy Tom's idea, spaceman. That guy gives me the creeps! He knows what's going to happen before it happens!"

Chief Pinkerton lumbered into view. "Very good!" he boomed. "It's nice to know you can do something useful. Now, remember what I said about inventing."

Jerry nodded. "Yes, sir. No spin, no bounce, no quiver!"

"Not even a tremble!"

Jerry snorted as he and Vic rode away. "Not even a tremble! Big deal!" But Vic was in no mood for jokes. "What's the matter, all-star?"

"I don't know. Something about that Happy Tom guy gives me the creeps. And then . . . aw, forget it!"

"And then what?"

"Well, Red is just a blowhard and I'm glad you stood up to him, Jerry, but you really did look sort of funny out there ducking that satellite gismo. Some of your inventions are pretty farfetched."

Jerry stared. His stomach suddenly felt like a tray full of ice cubes. "All I was trying to do was help Mr. Happy. Gosh, Vic, we both decided . . ."

"What do we know about that odd character? All his television cameras and radio recorders and that crazy transelastic stuff!"

"Transoplastic—and what's so crazy about it? You saw it yourself!"

"That's just it! He's got a whole big roomful of the stuff, but what's it good for?"

Jerry fumbled with his glasses. "It must have some use. Mr. Happy is no dummy. He wouldn't waste his time making something that was worthless!"

"I don't know if he would or not!"

"All right, we'll ask him. Come on!"

Vic shook his head. "I think I'll go practice some basketball."

Jerry twisted about. "You aren't going out to the lab?"

Vic shrugged. "Sometimes . . . well, sometimes I wish you were more interested in sports. I get tired of hearing all the guys make jokes about you. They're just kidding and all but . . ." He turned at the corner. "I'll see you tomorrow, spaceman."

"O.K., all-star." Jerry watched Vic pedal away. "Gosh, even when my automatic baseball-pitching machine tore the covers off all his new balls he didn't act like this." He bent forward, pushing hard against the pedals. "I think I'd better ask a few questions," he muttered, "and I think old 'Honest Abe' better have some answers!"

CHAPTER **5**

From some hidden loud-speaker the voice of Happy Tom Happy greeted Jerry as he stepped into the clapboard shack. "Stand in the middle of the room." The floor lowered with the familiar hissing noise. "Use the Visiospecs hanging on the post near the door."

Jerry zigzagged through the transoplastic. Apparently Mr. Happy had been expecting him. What was it Vic had said about this strange man knowing things were going to happen even before they did? By the time Jerry burst into the glittering laboratory his mind boiled with countless questions. "Mr. Happy," he blurted, "I'd like to ask . . . er . . ." He skidded to a stop.

Mr. Happy sat motionless, staring straight ahead. "Yes, that's it!" he said, apparently talking to the wall. He opened a drawer, withdrew a post card and began scribbling busily.

"Ahem," Jerry cleared his throat.

Mr. Happy glanced about. "Hello, Jerry. I'm playing Timecheck."

"Time what?"

"Timecheck. It's a little like checkers."

Jerry eyed the empty lab. "Who . . . who are you playing with?"

"Friend of mine in Australia. Here." Happy Tom held out the post card.

It was addressed to someone in Sidney, Australia. Jerry flipped it over. "D 5 dash 560 Red J 3 . . ." he read. "What's this?"

"That's my move. We send cards to each other once a week."

"Oh. Where's the . . . er . . . board?"

Mr. Happy tapped his head. "In here—all three of them."

"Three?"

The tall man made a little pencil drawing of what looked like three window screens, one above the other.

"Gosh," Jerry puzzled, "you sure must use a lot of checkers."

"Sixty-eight thousand, to be exact. But, of course, they aren't like regular checkers. Our markers look more like points of light in space. Each point can move forward or backward, like ordinary two-dimensional checkers, plus up and down, sideways and sort of slantwise at an angle."

Jerry whistled. "Sort of three-dimensional checkers."

55

"Four-dimensional," the tall scientist corrected. "Each move is based on the present plus the future divided by twice the square root of the past."

"Oh," Jerry nodded, "sure." He fumbled for his glasses, trying to remember some of the questions he was going to ask. Sixty-eight thousand points of light kept getting in his way. His thoughts were interrupted by a harsh buzzing.

"We have visitors," Mr. Happy murmured, as he strode toward the huge television. The long screen revealed the figures of three leather-coated young men astraddle motorcycles. Mr. Happy enlarged a section until the figures filled the space.

"Hey, those guys are part of that Black Angel bunch!" Jerry exclaimed. "Look at those fancy motorcycles—especially that one! It's covered with almost as many gadgets as your bicycle!"

"That's the reason they're here."

Jerry scratched his head. "I don't follow you."

"The fellow with the fancy jacket is actually jealous because my bicycle has more gadgets than his motorcycle."

"That's why they were giving you all that trouble," Jerry murmured, "until . . ." he paused, remembering what Vic had said about the mystery of the battered and bruised motorcyclists.

". . . until they met with an unfortunate accident?"

"Well, yes. After all, they were picking on you . . ."

"They were also racing in the streets of Saulito."

"What's that got to do with it?"

"Who would be annoyed with a gang of motorcyclists making trouble in Saulito?"

56

Jerry thought for a moment. "Chief Pinkerton?"

Happy Tom nodded. "A very strong and agile man despite his bulky appearance. Several of the Black Angels discovered this the hard way when they tried to jump him one night."

"Well," Jerry told himself, "that answers one question. Funny how simple the truth can be."

Mr. Happy bent to adjust a knob on the control panel. The voices of the leather-coated trio filled the lab.

". . . where he lives, Buck?" the smallest of the three was squeaking.

"Yeah," the one with the fancy motorcycle snarled, "and there ain't no fat cops around neither!"

Sounds just like Red Davis, Jerry thought, then he turned. "Mr. Happy, I want to thank you for helping me this afternoon. If you hadn't called the Fire Department I might still be out there wrapped around that pole. I guess using satellites for advertising wasn't such a good idea."

Happy Tom shook his head. "I think it's a good idea, Jerry." Then he bent to fiddle with the control panel again.

". . . and break the windows," another of the trio was saying.

"I'm going to break more than windows, Skinhead," the one called Buck snarled. "I'm going to break me some teeth. Come on, you guys."

Mr. Happy flicked a stray lock of hair from his forehead. A sudden sparkle in his black eyes betrayed his solemn expression.

Like Indians attacking a wagon train, the motorcyclists

charged forward and began circling the shack. Dust, dirt and the roar of motors filled the air.

Over the racket Jerry could hear Buck shouting, "Hey, Long John, come on out. I want to talk to you!"

"Yeah," the smallest of the three echoed, "come on out and be friendly!"

Suddenly Buck skidded to a stop in front of the door. He leaned across his handle bars. "Don't be scared, slim, we might even buy some ice cream from ya!" His words sent the others into fits of laughter. "Make mine vanilla," Buck bellowed.

"Hey, maybe he ain't home," the smallest broke in.

"Aw, he's in there, all right, Shorty . . . probably hiding in a corner!"

Jerry glanced away from the screen to find Mr. Happy calmly measuring chemicals at his workbench. "What if these three characters decide to break into your shack?"

Happy Tom finished a careful measurement and clamped the flask above a Bunsen burner. "They probably will," he murmured.

Jerry gulped, then twisted back to the TV.

Buck was swaggering toward the door. "Hey, Slim Jim, if you don't come out I'm gonna be very unhappy!"

Jerry noted that the blustering hoodlum waited until his companions joined him before he made his next move.

"O.K., meathead, now you've made me mad! I ain't gonna buy your ice cream—I'm going to bust right in and take it!" Buck threw his shoulder against the door. A look of surprise flashed over his ugly face when the door swung open at his touch.

58

The two other cyclists crowded forward and out of range of the television cameras.

Mr. Happy pressed a button on the control panel. A central section of the giant screen flickered, faded, then came on again, revealing the inside of the shack.

Buck was standing in the middle of the room. "Look under the bed," he ordered.

"Nobody here," Shorty announced.

"Maybe he went out the window," Skinhead suggested. He rattled the window frames. "Nah, they're all locked."

"Ain't that a shame. Left his 'Home, Sweet Home' wide open. We ought to teach him a lesson."

"Sure thing, Buck. We can bust it up a little!"

"Ain't only going to bust it up a *little*, Shorty!"

"You ain't thinking of using that dynamite?"

"Why not? Teach old Slim Jim a real good lesson."

As the blustering Buck turned toward the door, Mr. Happy flicked a switch. The door slammed shut.

Buck rattled the doorknob. "What the . . ." he blurted. Then he clamped his hands over his ears as if he were trying to shut out a loud noise.

Jerry pressed forward. Even his ears tingled. "What is it?"

"Ultrasonic high-frequency whistle," Mr. Happy explained.

"Ultrasonic," Jerry repeated, rubbing his ears. Then he understood. It was a whistle, too high even to be heard, yet powerful enough to be painful to the ears.

"It's only at ten now," Mr. Happy explained, pointing to a gauge. "At fifty their eardrums would burst."

59

As it was, all three of the Black Angels were frantically clawing at their ears as they shoved against the door.

Suddenly another figure flashed on the screen.

"Look, it's Vic! He's riding up to the shack!" Jerry caught Mr. Happy's arm. "He's going to walk right into the middle of them!"

"Calm down." The tall man flicked a switch. The needle swung back to zero.

"What was that?" Buck bellowed, shaking his head.

"Gas!" Shorty squeaked. "Some sort of gas!"

"Let's get outa here!" Skinhead screamed. In the next instant the desperate man hurled the table through a window. All three bolted for the opening. With the aid of his knees and elbows, Buck was first out. Skinhead was next. Shorty, bent double from a well-placed elbow, staggered about gasping for breath. "Wait . . . wait . . ." His buddies paid no heed. Intent on saving their own skins, they scrambled around the corner and were clambering onto their cycles when they spotted a bewildered Vic.

Jerry twisted about to find himself alone.

Mr. Happy's voice came from his apartment. "Put on your Visiospecs. I'll be with you as soon as I find something."

Jerry slipped the heavy goggles into place just as Happy Tom reappeared. But he wasn't carrying a gun or a club or even a rock! Instead he had a small book in his hands and seemed to be reading it. "Follow me!" he snapped.

They zigzagged through the transoplastic and through a door Jerry hadn't noticed before. It opened onto a narrow, sloping passageway. Striding ahead, the tall scientist continued to read his book as calmly as if they were out for a stroll in the park. They came up out of the tunnel in the middle of the eucalyptus grove. Jerry caught sight of the title of the book: *Jujitsu: Japanese Art of Self-defense.*

Mr. Happy continued his reading, leafing through the pages and murmuring, "Well, well."

Jerry trotted alongside. "Good time for a little review, eh?" he joked, trying not to stumble over his own shaking knees.

"Review?" Mr. Happy glanced up. "Oh, no, I've always wanted to learn jujitsu, but just couldn't find the time. . . ."

"You . . . you're just learning . . . now?"

Happy Tom shrugged. "I really should take a little more time, but this is an emergency." He went back to reading as they rounded the corner of the shack.

Shorty, still puffing from the effects of Buck's elbow, was just now boosting himself through the window. Without breaking his stride, Mr. Happy shifted the book from his right to his left hand and delivered a short, chopping blow to Shorty's neck. The cyclist flipped out of the window and slammed to earth. Except for a slight twitch in his left foot, he lay perfectly still.

Then Jerry spotted Vic standing with feet apart and fists clenched. Buck slouched facing him. His thumbs were caught "tough guy" fashion in the back pockets of his denims. "Watza matta," he slurred, "this yer no talk day? Grab him, Skinhead!"

But Skinhead was much too busy watching the approach of Happy Tom to grab anything except the handle

bars of his motorcycle. This didn't help, however. Happy Tom shouldered Buck to one side, caught the wild-eyed Skinhead by the front of his jacket and flipped him headlong into the shack.

As Buck spun to face the tall man, Vic dropped nimbly to his knees. A slight shove on the part of Happy Tom sent the gaping cycle jockey toppling backward. He greeted the earth with a jarring thud.

Vic straightened and stepped to one side. "Hello, Mr. Happy!" he grinned with new respect. "Glad to see you!"

"Here," Happy Tom tossed his book, "you might find this interesting."

"Look out!" Jerry shouted. But no sooner had Buck scrambled to his feet than he was slammed to earth. A look of fear spread across his ugly, piglike face. He rolled over and scuttled on hands and knees toward his motorcycle. Mr. Happy brought him to his feet by the scruff of his neck, then flipped him earthward once more.

Jerry glanced at the sleeping Skinhead. "Three up and three down," he giggled. "Buck, Skinhead and . . ." He gulped. Shorty was no longer sprawled beneath the window. Jerry scampered around the corner. The wobbly cyclist was swinging aboard his machine.

"Hey, Slim Jim," Shorty squeaked, stamping his powerful engine into life, "I'm going to grind you into hamburger!" Then he pushed off and came roaring like a maddened bull directly toward Vic and Mr. Happy.

"Oh, my gosh, what'll I do?" Jerry fumbled for his glasses. His fingers brushed against the Visiospecs hanging around his neck. "Hey, maybe . . ." He spun and dashed

64

toward the eucalyptus trees. The angry rasp of Shorty's cycle echoed in the narrow tunnel as Jerry scurried through it.

Shorty was skidding about in a tight turn as Jerry popped up into sunlight again. The skinny little cyclist had managed to flush his quarry. Vic crouched twenty feet from the safety of the shack. Jerry staggered out into the open.

Shorty's face cracked into a triumphant leer. "I'm going to get one of you! I can't miss!"

"Come on, stumpy," Jerry yelled, "let's play bullfight. You be the bull; you're the ugliest!"

Shorty revved his motor. Dirt churned from his back wheel. He shot forward.

"Move around, Jerry!" Vic gasped, "Move around! Don't just stand there!"

But Jerry stood motionless as if he were posing for a snapshot. "Wait, wait, wait!" he told himself. The charging cycle grew larger and larger. The blast of its motor seemed to shake the ground. Jerry stood an instant longer "Now!" He doubled over, fell to one side and rolled.

The leering Shorty sailed by. His motorcycle, however, did not. It flipped, back wheel over front, and crunched to the ground upside down. Fenders, headlights, handle bar grips and parts of the motor flew out of the dust.

Vic ran to Jerry's side. "Man oh man, I thought you were a goner!" Jerry was still on his knees. He seemed to be looking for something. "What's the matter, you hurt?"

Jerry glanced up. "No, no, it's the transoplastic. I put it right here."

"Man, that Shorty sailed twenty feet . . ."

"But it's gone!"

"Huh? What's gone?"

"The block of transoplastic. That's what Shorty ran into. But it's disappeared. Here, take the Visiospecs and look for yourself."

Vic bent forward and peered through the goggles. "Nothing here but a pile of some kind of dust."

Happy Tom's angry voice cut across Vic's words. The tall man was standing over Buck and the now-awake Skinhead. "Get on your cycles and clear out of here! If I catch you on my property again you'll think what happened this time was a picnic!"

The bedraggled cyclists struggled to their feet, draped a limp and babbling Shorty across the fender of Skinhead's motorcycle and wobbled away.

Jerry and Vic helped Mr. Happy return the table inside the shack. While the tall man inspected the broken window, Jerry whispered, "I'm glad you decided to come, even though you did walk smack-dab into a big mess!"

"It was worth it just to see Happy Tom flip those guys around! He's a real expert at jujitsu. And look, he gave me his book!"

Jerry decided not to tell Vic how much time it had taken Happy Tom to become a jujitsu expert. "Yeah, sure thing, but what made you change your mind, all-star?"

"Well, I was over at the gym shooting basketballs and all of a sudden it hit me."

"The ball?"

"No, funny man, an idea for using transo-whatchama-

66

callit. How about transparent basketball backboards? You could see right through it! And transparent backstops for baseball diamonds!"

"Hey, you really did have a brainstorm, didn't you?"

"You haven't even heard the best one. How about a giant trans . . . transo . . . how about a great big bowl of this stuff three hundred feet high—and long enough to cover a football field! You could play football any time and never worry about rain or snow or anything!"

"Hey, all-star, you've been thinking overtime!"

"Sure!" Vic stepped closer. "You know this Happy Tom guy isn't so odd after all. Nothing odd about the way he threw those loudmouthed cycle jockeys around. And you know something else, spaceman—guys who make fun of other people usually can't do anything themselves!"

Happy Tom finished his window inspection. "Let's all go down to the lab," he suggested. "All this excitement calls for ice cream 'on the house.' "

Jerry perched atop a workbench spooning a chocolate sundae. "Mr. Happy, when Shorty ran into that piece of transoplastic, it sort of crumbled to dust."

The tall man finished adjusting a network of glass tubes. "Transoplastic is tough, but it does crumble under a strong enough shock."

Vic glanced up from his "Butterscotch Delight." "Another thing, Mr. Happy, how come that elevator works when you say those numbers?"

"The elevator and sliding panels work by sound, Vic. The numbers I speak are like the numbers you dial for a combination lock."

Jerry jumped down and ran his finger tips over some of the glittering equipment. "Why did you come to Saulito in the first place?"

"I need a special type of sand to make T-36. There are only two places in the world where it is easily available. Oddly enough, Saulito is one of them."

"Special sand, eh?" Vic quizzed. "What does it look like?"

"You wouldn't be able to tell it from ordinary sand, Vic, unless you were trained to know the difference. Anyway, I used the last of it yesterday."

"Huh? You mean you can't make any more transo . . . whatchamacallit?"

The tall scientist nodded.

"But you said there were two places where you could get the sand," Jerry quizzed. "Where's the other one?"

"In Africa."

Vic whistled. "Africa? I guess that means you have to sell what you have before you can make any more. Hey, spaceman, we've got to get going on this presentation!"

Jerry grinned. "Check, all-star. Let's blast off for my lab. I've got a few things cooking there!"

"If you're going through town would you mail this card?" Mr. Happy picked up the post card addressed to his Timecheck opponent.

"Yes, sir. Slip on your Visiospecs, muscles. Let's blast!"

Vic turned as they pedaled away from the shack. "What's on that card Mr. Happy gave you?"

Jerry decided to go slow. Something as strange as four-dimensional checkers might send Vic back to the basketball court. "It's a sort of code . . . to somebody in Australia."

"Code? What kind of a code?"

"It describes a move in a . . . a game he and this Australian play."

"You mean like when two guys play chess by mail?"

"Yes, that's it. Only it's checkers."

"Checkers!" Vic snorted. "I'll bet old 'Honest Abe' doesn't play just regular, old-fashioned checkers!"

Jerry bit his lip. It seemed time to change the subject. "Boy, your idea about a transoplastic football stadium is the greatest, all-star!"

"Uh-huh," Vic nodded. "Checkers, eh? I once read about some guy who played checkers without using a board. I'll bet that's what Happy Tom does."

"As a matter of fact, Happy Tom plays checkers on three boards at once and still doesn't actually have a board!"

"Just as I thought . . . a Grade A, Number One, triple decker checker game, all right! Probably take an ordinary person thirteen years just to learn the rules. Yes, sir, that Happy Tom is an amazing guy!"

"Check!" Jerry grinned.

"I'll come over to Proctor's tomorrow morning to meet you," Vic shouted, as Jerry turned into the alley. "We'll get going in high gear on this thing!"

Jerry waved. "Looks like the world of sports is going to be minus one all-star," he giggled, "while Victor Lathrop, Boy Supersalesman, goes to work!"

CHAPTER 6

Mr. Barnes rustled the morning newspaper. "Mr. Proctor tells me you're doing a fine job."

"The way I have it figured," Jerry grinned, "I'm replacing his window at about three square inches per day." He swallowed another spoonful of "Atompep," the breakfast cereal shaped like little atoms.

Peggy, Jerry's pretty sister, glanced up from a letter she was reading. "Mary Ann says she's having a wonderful time at summer camp. And Mary Ann's brother is taking dancing lessons."

Jerry snorted, "Dancing lessons!"

"At least," Peggy snapped in her best "older sister" tone, "he's learning something valuable, instead of going around shooting newspapers through windows!"

"Valuable? What's so valuable about learning to dance? What's there to dance with except a bunch of giggling girls?"

"Peggy! Jerry!" Mrs. Barnes broke in.

Mr. Barnes folded his paper and stood up. "Do you want to ride with me this morning, Jerry?"

"Yes, sir. As a matter of fact, I've got something I'd like to tell you."

As Mr. Barnes backed down the driveway, Jerry was busy trying to figure a way he could talk about Happy Tom without disclosing the secret of Formula T-36. He decided to simply tell the truth, which usually turned out to be the easiest way. "Have you seen that tall, sad-faced man who sells ice cream? He has a bicycle covered with all kinds of gadgets."

Mr. Barnes nodded. "Yes, I've seen him."

"Well, he lives in a little shack out on Railroad Street near the gravel pit. That is, everybody thinks he lives in the shack. But a couple days ago Vic and I were . . . er . . . snooping around this little shack and he caught us."

"Snooping?"

"We weren't doing anything wrong. We were just sort of looking in the window and things. Well, anyway, he caught us." Jerry paused. "From now on, Dad, this gets to be sort of secret. You won't tell anyone?"

"I promise."

"Well, Mr. Happy—that's the ice cream man's name—has a huge storage room and a lab and a neat little apartment, all underground beneath this shack. Mr. Happy is a scientist . . . matter of fact, he's a genius."

Mr. Barnes grunted. "Underground, you say?"

"That's right, and it's all fixed up with radio-recording alarms and giant TV screens and ultrasonic whistles . . ."

"Do you remember if your mother asked me to bring something home tonight?"

"No, I didn't hear her say . . . hey, you're not listening!"

"Certainly I am. You're going to build an underground shack with a giant radio out by the gravel pit."

"No, Dad, it's Mr. Happy and he already has this underground lab. You see, the floor of the shack is really an elevator . . ."

"Here's Proctor's, son. Are you certain your mother didn't tell me to bring something home?"

Jerry shrugged. "I didn't hear her say anything, Dad. Thanks for the ride." He jumped out of the car. "I don't think I got through to him. But then, shacks with elevators and underground labs with giant TV's do sound a little farfetched."

Three hours and some four square inches of window glass later, Jerry wrestled the last of several cardboard boxes into place. He paused to look about. What had been a hodgepodge of crates, boxes and junk was now an orderly storeroom. Jerry couldn't help a little puff of pride. "G. Barnes," he chuckled, "boy businessman!" Then he turned and hurried down the stairs.

"The big room is all finished, Mr. Proctor," he announced. "I'll start on the little one tomorrow."

The tall businessman smiled. "You're doing fine, Gerald."

72

Just then Vic appeared. "Hi, spaceman."

"Hi, all-star. I'll see you tomorrow, Mr. Proctor. Goodby."

"Have you thought of anything?" Vic questioned, as he pushed his bike along the sidewalk. "I had a brainstorm about staging an exhibition baseball game but I can't figure how we could work in that transostuff."

Jerry shook his head. "My mind's a blank. Everything I think of moves."

Vic snorted. "That would go over like a cast-iron balloon."

"Look, what's that?" Jerry was pointing to a large truck and trailer piled high with brightly painted poles and frames.

"Probably part of the carnival for the fair."

"I'd forgotten all about the fair." Jerry fumbled with his glasses. "That would be the perfect place to present transoplastic. Let's get over to the library, Vic. Maybe we can find an idea or two."

"Check!"

The Saulito Public Library was actually the top floor of an ancient two-story building. It looked shabby compared to the sparkling gas station near by. Yet, old as it was, Jerry could usually find answers to his questions there. "That's more than you can do in a gas station," he said to himself, as they climbed the creaking stairs.

Mrs. Catlin, the friendly librarian, nodded in silent greeting.

As usual, Vic made a beeline for the books on sports. Jerry began to browse along the science shelves. It wasn't long before he found a book and an idea. It was a reference book but Mrs. Catlin always had paper and pencil handy. Jerry scribbled busily.

Vic walked to his side. "What's up?"

"Wait a minute," Jerry murmured. "There!" He pushed the book toward his friend. "Look at this, all-star!"

"*Harmless Tricks with Chemistry,*" Vic read. "Hey, this sounds great! Can we do it?"

"Sure, I have it all written down. Let's blast!"

Jerry returned the book to its place and gave Mrs. Catlin a smile and her pencil.

"The best thing about it, spaceman, is that it won't move," Vic laughed as they tramped down the stairs. "Not a quiver!"

Mr. Lester, the elderly druggist, looked out from his little prescription room as Jerry approached. "Hello, Gerald, Vic."

"Hi, Mr. Lester." Jerry held out his penciled notes. "Can we buy these chemicals?"

The old druggist tilted his head. "Hummm. Yes, yes, all except this one. You'd have to bring a note from your parents before I could sell you this. It's too dangerous. Say, what are you planning?"

The kind old druggist was always eager to learn about his schemes, but this time Jerry shook his head. "Top secret, Mr. Lester. I'm sorry."

The man nodded with a disappointed pout. "How much do you want to buy?"

74

Jerry dug into his pockets. The best he could do was three pennies and a wooden nickel from the grand opening of a supermarket. "Have you any loot, Vic?"

Vic pulled out his wallet, opened the top, pushed back a flap, unsnapped a secret compartment and unzipped a secret secret pocket. He produced a tightly folded one-dollar bill. "I've been saving 'George' here but this is a good cause."

The druggist nodded. "A dollar's worth? All right. I'll put each ingredient into a separate envelope and label them." This completed, he handed Jerry the little bundles. "There's more than a dollar's worth here, but we can't let a little thing like money get in the way of inventing."

"Gosh, thanks very much, Mr. Lester."

A short time later, Vic danced impatiently as Jerry poked through the jumble beneath his workbench. "Come on, spaceman, let's get this show on the road!"

"O.K., all-star, bring over that big piece of tin. We'll put it over the bench, just to be doubly safe."

With Vic's help, Jerry completed the preparations. The bench was cluttered with tin cans, old empty pie plates, battered pots and pans and an inverted hubcap. Jerry studied his notes. "Now, let's see, three parts of this and one level teaspoon . . . hey, we need a teaspoon!" He laid the notes on the bench. "Wait here a second, I'll get one in the kitchen."

Mrs. Barnes looked up as Jerry came in. "Will you go to the store for me? I need some baking powder."

"Right now?"

"Please, I'm in the middle of a cake."

"Cake!"

"Chocolate cake. The money's on the table."

Jerry scooped up the coins. "Say no more." He followed his "fast route"—through the next door neighbor's hedge, over a low fence and into the back entrance of the grocery. He returned the same way.

"Thank you, Jerry. What are you . . ." The ringing of the telephone interrupted Mrs. Barnes's question. "I'll get it."

Jerry pulled open a drawer and began to paw over the contents, looking for a spoon old and battered enough for his purposes. He half listened to his mother's cheery greeting. "Hello, Mrs. Miller, how nice . . . what? Smoke . . . on fire!" Jerry was paying close attention now; so much so that he slammed the drawer shut on his finger. "Ouch! Fire . . . what's on fire?"

Mrs. Barnes hurried past him. "That was Mrs. Miller. She says it's on fire!"

"What?"

"The garage!"

"Oh, my gosh!" Jerry bounded for the door.

Great clouds of smoke were billowing from the garage.

Vic's in there! Jerry thought, with a jab of panic. Then, just as quickly, he skidded to a stop. His mother nearly piled into him.

"What . . ." she demanded. "Jerry, don't just stand there, get the hose! Perhaps we can . . ."

Jerry held up his hand. "Wait a minute, Mom, it's all right. There's no fire."

76

"No fire? Why the smoke is just pouring out!"

"I can explain. It's very simple." Jerry cocked his head, then moaned, "Oh, no, not again!"

Mrs. Barnes had heard the sirens, too. "Mrs. Miller said she called the Fire Department." She turned. "Just what do you mean by no fire? If that garage burns down . . ."

"Honest, the garage isn't going to burn down. Nothing is going to burn down. Look at the smoke, it's colored. Vic is just stirring up a few experimental smoke bombs. Beautiful, isn't it?" Jerry couldn't help but admire the swirls of multicolored smoke; especially a lovely yellow-green plume floating from a side window. His admiration was short lived, however. In the next minute the familiar red Saulito fire truck lumbered into view. Behind it bounced the captain's car. Fire Captain Towne, a slightly built man and probably the most polite fire captain in the whole world, bounded from the car. Jerry darted forward and met him at the garage door.

The slender man peered through a wisp of violet smoke. "Well, well, hello there, Jerry. What seems to be the trouble here?"

Jerry wasn't surprised at this cordial greeting. He had seen Captain Towne at some real big fires and the man always acted as if he were at a church picnic.

"Nothing really," Jerry exclaimed. "Vic is inside doing some exper . . ."

"Victor is inside, you say?"

"Yes, sir. You see we were at the library today and . . ."

"Please excuse me, Gerald." The fire captain gestured

77

toward a tall, rubber-coated fireman. "There is a boy in-side, Johnson. I think it might be a good idea if you would bring him out."

"Yes, sir!" the tall fireman snapped. He shouldered his way past Jerry and through the door. An instant later he reappeared. "Forgot my gas mask," he murmured sheep-ishly. With a bulb-nosed gas mask in place, he tramped into the smoke once more.

Jerry could see Vic's outline through the multicolored curtain. He was still mixing and so busy, it would seem, that he hadn't even heard the sirens.

Fireman Johnson groped toward the workbench. Jerry heard his muffled words. "Hullo thur."

Vic jumped. His voice was clear. and strong. "What the . . . my gosh, you scared me! What do you want? Why are you wearing that mask?"

"Smuk!"

"What?"

"Smuk! Smuk!"

"Oh, smoke. Pretty, isn't it? Why don't you come over here by the window where it's clear. Hey, what are you doing? Put me down!"

"Ruscooing yuh!"

"What? I wish you'd take that thing off!"

There was a pause while Fireman Johnson pulled off his mask. "I'm rescuing you. Just be calm while I throw you over my shoulder."

"Throw me where? But I don't want to be rescued. Honest, I'm O.K. . . ."

78

"Oh, I'm sorry but you'll just have to be rescued. It's my job."

"Hey, look, I've just got a few more things to mix. Why don't you come back in about five minutes, then I'll be ready to be rescued."

"Just stay right there. I'll be back." Fireman Johnson reappeared for the second time. "There's a boy in there, all right, Cap'n Towne, but he doesn't want to be rescued."

Fire Captain Towne took off his white helmet and scratched his head. "Well, this is problem. I'm afraid you're going to have to insist, Clarence. We have the reputation of our department to think of."

"Yes, sir!" Fireman Johnson tramped into the smoke again. "I'm just going to have to rescue you, son. Cap'n's orders."

"Even if I don't want to be rescued?"

"Aw, come on, I might lose my job. Be a good boy and let me rescue you."

"Gee, I never looked at it that way. Sure, just a sec. O.K."

Jerry stepped back as Fireman Johnson came staggering from the garage with Vic draped across his shoulder. It looked like a very heroic rescue, except for the can Vic was holding and the billowing pink smoke that poured from it.

"Hi, Jerry," Vic grinned. He jiggled the can. "How do you like this?"

Fireman Johnson steadied himself and set Vic on his

feet. Then he heaved a sigh of relief and wandered off toward the truck.

"Thank you," Vic called after him, "and thank you, Captain Towne. Can I go back in now?"

"Perhaps you'd better wait until the smoke clears a little." The captain turned and murmured some polite orders to the truck driver. The fire truck roared to life and backed away.

"I'm sorry you had to come all the way . . ." Jerry's mother began.

Mrs. Miller interrupted in an excited voice, "I called you! I saw all that smoke! It was just pouring out!"

Fire Captain Towne doffed his white helmet. "That's perfectly all right, ladies. It's our job, you know. And I don't mind telling you that we of the Saulito Fire Department look forward to answering calls that have to do with Gerald Barnes. It keeps us on our toes. Like the other day . . . what other fire department, even in a large city, could ever hope to be called to stop a runaway satellite?"

Jerry glanced at his mother. "I . . . er . . . I guess I forgot to tell you about that."

Vic broke in. "It's my fault. Jerry went in to find a spoon but I had already found one so I went right ahead and, first thing I know, here is this man with a gas mask trying to throw me over his shoulder."

"You see?" Captain Towne chuckled. "Really keeps us on our toes. Now, if you'll excuse me, ladies. Do come and visit us . . . open house between one and three. Good afternoon."

Mrs. Barnes turned. "Would you like to come in for a

80

cup of coffee, Mrs. Miller? And as for you, young man, I'll talk to you this evening!"

Jerry winced. A "young man" type talk wasn't something he looked forward to. "Oh, well," he shrugged, after his mother had slammed the back screen, "at least the smoke looked real great."

"Do you think we can use it?"

"Why not? Let's go out to Happy Tom's and see what he thinks."

"Check!"

Halfway out Railroad Street Jerry suddenly pulled up short. "Wouldn't that frost you!"

Vic skidded to a stop. "What's the trouble?"

Jerry glanced up. "Flat tire. I didn't even see that broken bottle."

Vic pushed backward. "It's only flat on the bottom, old buddy."

"Very funny. I guess I'll have to push it all the way back to town."

"Maybe Happy Tom has some supersonic patches, spaceman. He has everything else."

"Could be, but if he doesn't I'd just have to push this crate twice as far."

Vic swung off his bike. "Here, we can ride double. Balance your bike alongside."

"Sure you can stand the extra strain, faint heart?"

Vic pushed off. "Just call me muscles!"

"O.K., muscles." Jerry struggled to keep his weaving bike upright as they bounced along. "Too bad you don't have an overhead rack, muscles. I could just pack my bike topside."

"With you on it," Vic snorted. "G. Barnes and his Flying Bicycle!"

"Flying bicycle . . . flying bicycle!" Jerry straightened. "Vic, that's it!" He reached for his glasses.

"Watch your bike!"

Vic's warning came too late. With a clatter, Jerry's bike lurched sideways, spilling them into the gravel.

"What an idea!" Jerry bubbled from where he sat. "I can see it now!" He spread his arms.

Vic stumbled to his feet, brushing dirt from his hair. "You can see what? What are you talking about?"

"A flying bicycle, all-star, a fabulous flying bicycle!"

"You didn't land on your head, did you?"

Jerry looked around. "Oh, I guess I forgot to hold onto my bike." He stood and rubbed the seat of his pants. "But it was worth it, all-star. It will be the greatest!"

"It better be, whatever it is! You almost broke my neck!" Vic bent to pull the bikes apart. "Now will you tell me what you're talking about?"

Jerry sidesaddled once again. "Like I said, a flying bicycle. Just imagine Happy Tom's bike . . . gadgets, noisemakers and all, soaring into the sky!"

"I still don't get you."

"We'll build a sort of bridge . . . a high . . . ramp out of transoplastic. Then old 'Honest Abe' will ride onto this ramp, which is invisible and . . ."

"Yeah, I get it! When he rolls over this transostuff it

83

will look like he's riding in mid-air! Man oh man, Jerry, that's a real Grade A, Number One, triple decker idea!"

"Triple decker!" Once more Jerry reached for his glasses. Once more his bike wobbled unattended. This time it was Vic who landed in a sitting position. Jerry sprawled face first. "Triple decker!" he sputtered. "We can use our bikes, as well as Happy Tom's. It will be the biggest thing since Tarzan invented apes! Happy Tom Happy's Fabulous Triple Decker Flying Bicycle!"

Vic joined in the chorus, waving his arms. "And each one of us can carry a different colored smoke bomb. Man oh man, it will be the . . ."

"Are you boys going to sit there shouting all day?" The man who spoke was leaning out of the window of a pickup. "I'd like to get by if you don't mind."

Jerry jumped to his feet. "Yes, sir! We . . . we just had a little spill."

Vic was busy separating the tangled bikes. "That's right, a little spill. There now, you can get by."

The man rolled forward with a puzzled grunt.

Jerry giggled. "At least he didn't run over us!"

Vic picked up his bike. "Suppose you just push your bike the rest of the way, spaceman. You might have another brainstorm and I'm too young to die."

"O.K., all-star," Jerry grinned. "I can hardly wait to tell Happy Tom about the Fabulous Flying Bicycle!"

"The Fabulous Triple Decker Flying Bicycle," Vic corrected, "with smoke screen attached!"

CHAPTER 7

"Great gyrating gyroscopes!" Jerry shouted. "It's the greatest!"

"Once more around my shack," Happy Tom directed from the topmost deck of the sparkling new triple decker flying bicycle.

Vic, astraddle the lower deck, pushed powerfully on the pedals. The tall contraption swept past Jerry. He stepped back for a better look. The wheelless frames of both his and Vic's bikes gleamed under a bright new coat of enamel. A stout framework of shiny chrome held them in place above Mr. Happy's glittering bicycle. The framework also held a cluster of fluttering pennants fore and aft; eight whip aerials; a red, white and blue box for confetti and a yellow balloon launcher.

"The greatest!" Jerry repeated. "And with the technicolor smoke screen it will be even greater!" He ran forward to steady the triple decker as it rolled to a stop.

Mr. Happy climbed to the ground.

Vic swung off and patted the confetti box. "I hope Mr. What's-his-name at the fair thinks so when he sees it."

"So do I." Jerry began folding a large green-and-yellow, much-patched awning, another of Mr. Proctor's castoffs. "Let's ride part way, then we can cover the bike and walk the rest of the way."

Mr. Happy glanced at his watch. "If you're going to walk that far you'd better start now. Your appointment is at two."

Vic scampered into the shack and reappeared carrying a box of tin cans. "Smoke bombs! I'll take them along just in case."

Jerry clambered to the second deck. "What's the man's name?" he shouted, as Vic pushed off.

"Twilliger," Mr. Happy answered. "C. H. Twilliger, Director of Special Events."

It was three minutes before two when they walked through the entrance door of the Saulito County Fair Administration Building. Jerry led the way down a long hall. "Here it is," he whispered, pointing to the door labeled SPECIAL EVENTS. He turned the knob. "Here goes."

The door opened onto a small office. A young lady glanced up from a typewriter. "Yes?"

Jerry cleared his throat. "Could we speak with Mr. Hilliger?"

"Twilliger?"

87

"Yes, could we speak with him? It's about a special event."

"Your name?"

"Barnes."

The secretary rose and disappeared behind a door marked PRIVATE in lemon-colored letters.

Vic looked about the spotless room. "Man oh man, this is about the cleanest place I've ever seen! Look at those signs!"

Jerry glanced at the row of white framed mottoes that lined the far wall. "NEATNESS SPELLS SUCCESS," he read, "A NEAT MAN IS A GOOD MAN," and "KEEP YOUR HANDS BUSY AND YOUR WORKBENCH NEAT." He fought down a giggle when he thought of his own workbench.

Just then the secretary popped back into the room. "You may go in."

Jerry led the way into the director's office. Vic closed the door behind them.

Ten minutes later, the door opened. A great puff of purple smoke rolled out, followed by Vic, then Jerry.

"Thank you, Mr. Killiger." Jerry called back over his shoulder. "And thank you, too," he said to the bewildered secretary. It wasn't until they had pushed their way out the big entrance doors that he began to laugh. "Man oh man! Are we lucky!"

"You can say that again!" Vic set the box of smoke bombs on the steps and wiped his forehead. "I sure didn't think old Mr. Fussy in there would let us present the triple decker."

"Especially after you spilled that purple smoke bomb all over his clean desk!" Jerry laughed.

"Very funny, I'm sure. But what about the window you broke?"

Jerry shrugged. "It was the only way I could think of to get rid of the smoke. I wonder if he didn't say 'Yes' just to get rid of us? Oh, well, no matter. We can present the triple decker and on Opening Day, too!" He patted the tall contraption. "Let's blast for Happy Tom's lab. For once, we've got some good news to tell him."

"Sure thing!" Vic smiled. In the next instant a sound brought the corners of his mouth down. From somewhere behind them came the heavy cough of motorcycle motors. Vic twisted about. "Look, here they come!"

Motorcycles came roaring around the corner of the Administration Building. Two by two they flashed by.

". . . six-eight-ten," Jerry counted. "Hey, look, there's Skinhead and Shorty!"

"Man your battle stations!" Vic shouted above the roar. "Looks like trouble! Skinhead and Shorty are turning around! Listen, Jerry, if they start anything you take off with the triple decker. I'll try to hold them."

Jerry nodded. He searched the street. For once he would have been happy to see a shiny black-and-white squad car. All he saw was the two leather-coated cyclists skidding to a stop.

Vic shifted his weight like a fighter just before the bell rings.

Jerry reached for his glasses. He was trying to plot the best escape route. Then he took his glasses off. "Nuts," he breathed, "if they want to get at the triple decker they'll have to climb over both of us!"

There was a funny little smile on Skinhead's mouth. "Remember us?"

"Yes," Vic snapped. "Last time I saw you guys you both were flat on your backs!"

"He remembers us all right," Shorty grinned.

Skinhead slid off his cycle. "Where's Slim Jim?"

Vic squared about. "Look, if you're going to start something, why don't you quit fooling around and start it?"

"Touchy, ain't he?" Shorty chuckled.

Skinhead grinned. "We ain't gonna start nothin'. We just want to talk."

"Sure!" Vic's voice was edged with suspicion.

"Yeah. The guys in the Silver Pistons don't go for no rough stuff."

"Silver Pistons?" Jerry asked.

"It's a motorcycle club."

"What happened to the Black Angels?"

"There ain't no more Black Angels. All we ever got out of that outfit was lumps. The guys in the Pistons are real pros! They don't ride around racin' and showin' off—that's kid stuff. Right now we're practicin' for a Motorcycle Masquerade. Going to put it on during the fair. Some of those guys in the Pistons can really ride—tricks and stunts and all! That's why most of us joined the Silver Pistons."

"Except Buck," Shorty added.

"The guy with the real fancy motorcycle?" Jerry quizzed.

"Yeah, that's what we wanted to talk to you about. He's out to get even with you. You'd better watch out for that creep. He's off his rocker!"

"Thanks for the warning," Vic grinned. "We thought maybe you were going to give us a hard time because of what happened the other day."

Skinhead shrugged. "That's what we got from foolin' around with a creep like Buck. Well, we'd better shove off. See you."

The pair straddled their cycles and pushed away. Their engines throbbed powerfully.

"Didn't even gun their motors, Vic," Jerry observed. "I guess they finally wised up."

Vic nodded. "Like I always say, old buddy, the people who make the most noise usually can't do anything else!"

"One thing, though."

"What's that?"

"Well," Jerry began, slipping on his glasses, "I read somewhere that the meanest animal is usually the one who has been kicked out of his pack."

"Like a lone wolf?"

"Yes," Jerry muttered, glancing over his shoulder, "or a mad Buck!"

"Let's worry about that jerk if and when the time comes! Right now we've got to hustle. Only a week to go before the fair opens!"

"Roger!"

CHAPTER 8

The planet earth, distant and veiled by clouds, spun through the star-speckled heavens. There was a pinpoint flash of light. A rocket pierced the clouds and arced past the moon.

Jerry hunched forward as the spaceship streaked through a shower of glittering meteorites; then it was lost in a pocket of velvet-black space dust. Not until the brave little ship settled on Mars did Jerry relax. "What a deal," he muttered.

He craned his neck searching for the first faint signs of the comet that would next sweep across the twinkling backdrop. Something which sounded like the thumping on a door echoed through endless space. Jerry turned his head. A voice came from somewhere near the Big Dipper.

"Hey, spaceman, open up!"

It was Vic calling from outer space. Jerry ducked his head and carefully balanced the Universoscope on his workbench.

"What's the big secret?" Vic quizzed, stepping into the room.

"Secret?"

"The only time you lock your door is when you are working on some big, top-secret type thing."

Jerry walked to the workbench. "It's secret, all right, old buddy, but not mine." He pointed to a large metal object shaped like a deep-sea diver's helmet. "The greatest, all-star!"

Vic stared. "It's the greatest, all right, but what is it?"

"Happy Tom's Universoscope, old buddy." Jerry picked it up. "Just stick your head in there."

"Not me, pal! There's something inside, I can hear it!"

"Matter of fact, there's a whole universe inside here," Jerry said, as he lowered the buzzing helmet over his head. He raised it. "See? Go ahead, try it."

Vic cautiously stuck his head into the opening. "Hey, it has holes in it! No, they're stars! My gosh, it looks like the sky at night! But what are those little balls spinning around?"

"The planets, all-star—earth, moon, Mars, Venus, Jupiter—the works!"

"They're spinning around just like real! Hey, there's a comet! What a beauty! There's the Big Dipper and the North Star and the Milky Way! Man oh man, this *is* the greatest!"

94

Jerry busied himself at his workbench while Vic enjoyed a trip into space by way of Mr. Happy's miniature planetarium. "It works by electricity," he explained. "These dials are the controls. You just set them if you want to see the rocket flight or the eclipse of the moon or something like that."

"You know, Jerry, I don't see why Mr. Happy sells ice cream when he can make things like this."

"I asked him the same thing, all-star. He said that it took him nearly three years to build this one, so each Universoscope would cost about thirty-five thousand dollars!"

"Thirty-five grand! I guess that is pretty steep for a toy. Hey, I just about forgot what I came over to tell you. Old 'Honest Abe' hasn't been spending all his time building Universoscopes. I met him this morning and he was driving a big truck he had rented."

"A truck! What for?"

"To carry that transostuff. He's been building the ramp at the fairgrounds. If we help him tonight he thinks we can get the job done in plenty of time."

"Good deal, but every time I think of sailing over that ramp I get cold chills. Have you thought of all the things that could go wrong? We might even have a flat tire just about the time we get on the very tiptop!"

"Nothing has happened yet, spaceman, and we've been practicing for a week now!"

"But the ramp we've been practicing on is only about a third as tall as the one we're going to ride at the fair!"

"Let's worry about that when the time comes, faint

heart. I guess I'd better blast for home. Happy Tom said we should meet him at the main gate about seven."

"Roger, all-star. I'll be over at your place right after dinner."

At suppertime Jerry sat at the table poking listlessly at his food. His stomach felt the size of a walnut. He came down from an imaginary transoplastic ramp into Peggy's bubbling account of the great Mr. Greyhead, her summer drama club coach.

". . . then he told us about the time he opened in a big city back east," Peggy was saying. "He said the day before he was so frightened that his stomach . . ."

". . . felt like a walnut," Jerry interrupted.

"What? That's exactly what he said. How did you know?"

"Just lucky, I guess," Jerry shrugged, stabbing at a pea.

"Well, anyway, Mr. Greyhead said his stomach felt about as big as a walnut and that all he could think about was . . ."

". . . a flying bicycle," Jerry broke in.

". . . was a flying bicycle. No, that's not what he said! He said all he could think about was a loose board in the middle of the stage. He was sure that he was going to trip on it and tumble right into the big bass drum in the orchestra pit. It was so funny that Mary Jane and I giggled for an hour . . ."

"I don't think it's very funny."

"I wish you'd quit interrupting me, Jerry!"

"Huh?" Jerry straightened. "Oh, I'm sorry. May I be excused?"

96

His mother looked up. "You don't want dessert? Are you feeling well?"

Jerry nodded. "I feel fine, for someone with a stomach the size of a walnut."

"Don't worry, Jerry," Peggy offered. "It's perfectly normal to have stage fright. Mr. Greyhead says it makes your performance that much better."

"I wonder if Mr. Greyhead can ride a bicycle," Jerry moaned.

"I wonder if it is wise to let you go through with this exhibition or whatever it is," Mr. Barnes murmured, trying to control a smile. "First you won't tell us anything except that you're going to ride some sort of flying bicycle —and now you're turning into a nervous wreck!"

"Remember what Mr. Greyhead says, Dad; the worse I feel now, the better I'll do tomorrow."

"If you last that long," Peggy giggled.

"What time will you be back tonight, Jerry?" Mrs. Barnes asked.

"When we finish, Mom. I don't know how long it will take."

"I want you to call if it gets too late."

"I will, Mom," Jerry promised, as he scampered up the stairs. He snapped on the light in his room and fished a key out from behind some books on a shelf. Ignoring a sign which read: "DANGER! HIGH VOLTAGE— RADIOACTIVE—TOP SECRET" he unlocked his battered desk. He pawed through the jumble of science fiction magazines, drawings of yet-to-be-built inventions, used TV picture tubes, a collection of plastic-coated

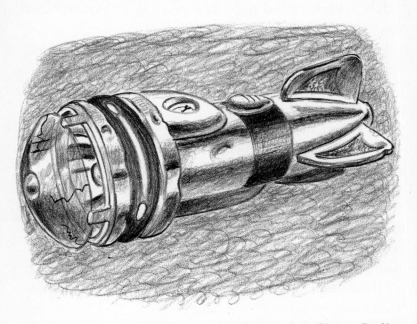

beetles, a pair of half-completed genuine Sioux Indian moccasins, wire, tin foil and assorted odds and ends. Finally, he brought out his Jet Cadet, infrared, compass-in-the-handle flashlight with a built-in Geiger counter. The needle of the compass was stuck at northeast. The infrared lens had several large cracks and the Geiger counter had long since made its last count. Jerry snapped the rocket-shaped switch. "Hummm, at least the light still works. Pretty good for three box tops and a quarter." He slammed the desk shut, replaced the key and scrambled downstairs.

"Don't forget to call if it gets too late, Jerry!"

"O.K., Mom."

Outside, Jerry tested his Jet Cadet Rocket Flash against

the soft blueness of the summer evening. The feeble beam fought its way bravely for about six feet, then seemed to lose courage.

Vic came to the door at the Lathrop house. "Come on in, spaceman, we're still eating."

"Hello, Jerry," jolly Mrs. Lathrop greeted. "Will you have a piece of cake?"

The short walk had somehow enlarged his stomach. "Thank you, Mrs. Lathrop," Jerry nodded, "maybe just a sliver."

Later, as he and Vic walked down the driveway, Jerry mused. "It's amazing how much a walnut can hold."

"Now, what have you got on your mind, besides dandruff?"

"You won't believe this, all-star, but a walnut can hold two pieces of cake and a glass of milk."

"Where did you learn all this?"

"At your place. I ate two pieces of cake and a glass of milk."

"What's that got to do with walnuts?"

"Every time I think of tomorrow my stomach shrinks to the size of a walnut . . . and I've been doing a lot of thinking lately!"

Vic snorted, "You, too? Do you know what Coach Moore says about pregame jitters?"

"I know what Mr. Greyhead says."

"Who's Mr. Greyhead?"

"Never mind. What does Coach Moore say about pregame jitters?"

"He says the best way to lose them is by running." Vic sprinted ahead with smooth strides.

"I was afraid he'd say something like that," Jerry puffed, as he straggled in pursuit. "Slow down a little and tell me what Mr. Happy said when you saw him this afternoon."

"He told me about building the ramp, like I said. He also mentioned something about using the truck tomorrow . . . said it would be a surprise, especially for you."

"Surprise?"

"That's what he said."

Jerry moaned. "As if I didn't have enough to think about."

CHAPTER 9

As usual, the night before opening day was a busy one at the fairgrounds. The air was filled with thumps, clatters, squeals and cackles. Pickup trucks rattled about busily. Workmen stepped in and out of little puddles of yellow light. A single cluster of field lights blazed in the black-purple sky over the grandstand. As if frightened by all the light and noise, the summer moon peeked timidly from behind the sign above the main gate.

Beneath the sign, near his guard shack, the paunchy, sour-faced gate guard stood glowering. "Get out of the driveway!" he commanded.

Jerry glanced at Vic with a shrug. During the busy fair week Mr. Campbell was about as friendly as a mad dog.

"Good evening, Mr. Campbell," Jerry grinned, playing

101

out his best line of soft soap. "How in the world do you keep track of all these trucks?"

The old guard waved a pickup through the gate, whacking it with his clipboard as it rolled by. "By not answering foolish questions!"

Vic stepped forward. "Did Mr. Happy speak to you about us?"

"Mr. Happy?" the guard growled. He paused to smack another truck with his clipboard. "Who's Mr. Happy?"

"He's . . . er . . . he's building something on the race track arena."

Mr. Campbell ran a stubby finger down the sheet of paper attached to his battered clipboard. "Happy, Happy, how do you spell it?"

"With an *h,*" Jerry offered, "like in hairless."

"Harrumph!" The baldheaded Mr. Campbell scowled. "Here 'tis. Oh, that feller! He's an odd one, he is!"

"Why?"

"Been goin' in and out all afternoon. In and out . . . in and out!"

"What's the matter with that?"

"Truck's empty when it goes in and empty when it comes out!" He slapped a passing pickup. "Waste of time!"

"Well, did Mr. Happy say anything about us?"

"Said you were his helpers. Must need lots of help with an empty truck. See for yourself . . . here he comes. Truck's empty, as usual."

Mr. Happy waved from the cab of an ancient, flat-bed truck. "Hop in," he directed.

102

Jerry climbed in beside Vic. "Thank you, Mr. Campbell," he called, as the truck rumbled through the gate.

"In and out . . . in and out!" the old guard muttered, taking an extra-vicious swipe at the "empty" truck. His clipboard whacked against something and flipped out of his hand. It bounced and came to rest seemingly in mid-air. Mr. Campbell's mouth dropped open.

"Hey," Jerry exclaimed, "stop a minute. We've got Mr. Campbell's clipboard." He scrambled out of the cab and onto the invisible load of transoplastic. Scooping up the clipboard, he thrust it into the still-outstretched hands of the bewildered man. "Drop something?"

Mr. Campbell's eyes darted from his board to Jerry, who appeared to be floating some four feet above the truck bed. "Down . . ." he wheezed, "d-down . . . down from the air, there!"

Jerry took a step forward.

"No, no, no! Don't come closer! You there . . . in the air . . . there!"

"In the air where?" Jerry giggled, doing a little dance.

"In the air, there!" The guard's face paled as Vic came traipsing across the blocks.

"Mr. Happy said we could ride back here," Vic whispered.

Jerry took his place at the end of the load, legs dangling. "Good-by, Mr. Campbell."

"Don't work too hard," Vic added.

The old guard gurgled something.

Jerry braced himself as they jiggled along. "Poor Mr. Campbell."

"Serves him right!" Vic snorted. "He's such a sour old lemon!"

Jerry waved at a workman. The man threw down his hammer. "That does it!" Jerry heard him mutter. "I'm going home! I've been working so hard I'm seeing flying boys!"

Two painters stepped out from a doorway as the truck lurched by. "What color are we going to paint the back wall?" one of them was asking.

"Mid-air!" the first stammered, as he stared at the truck.

"Mid what?"

"Both of them . . . mid-air!"

"What's that, sort of a blue?"

Jerry didn't hear the answer. The truck slowed, turned and rumbled into a narrow tunnel in the grandstand.

The tunnel guard was slouched sleepily on a tilted chair. He thumbed the truck through, glanced at Jerry and Vic, looked again and tumbled backward with a grunt of surprise.

The truck rolled across the dirt track, jounced onto the grass-covered arena inside and jolted to a stop. Both Jerry and Vic jumped to the ground to examine a tall framework of metal pipes. Jerry took a second look and noticed that the grass at one side of the framework was pressed down into a long, narrow furrow. He stepped forward and waved his hands over the matted grass. His finger tips collided with smooth solidness.

Mr. Happy stepped to his side. "Here, use these Visio-specs."

Jerry quickly slipped on the heavy goggles. He stared up at the nearly completed ramp, shimmering blue-green behind the network of pipes. "It's a mile high! Just looking at it gives me goose pimples!"

"You can say that again!" Vic chortled, adjusting his goggles. "It sure is pretty. Gosh, Mr. Happy has really been working hard. Except for that section on the top, it looks finished."

The tall, sad-faced scientist was busy unloading glowing blocks from the truck onto a small elevator built into the framework. Jerry and Vic hurried to join him.

The work went smoothly. After the first elevator load, Mr. Happy and Vic stayed high atop the framework while Jerry worked below. Load after load whizzed up the little cable-operated lift. The blocks weren't heavy by themselves, but as Jerry set the last one in place he could feel tight knots in his muscles. He balanced himself on the little platform. "That's it!" he grinned, as the elevator jolted to a stop.

Vic straightened. "Good deal!"

Mr. Happy nodded. He was holding what looked to be an oilcan with a long spout and a trigger attached to the handle. As Vic held a block in place, Happy Tom ran the nozzle of the spout along the edges, triggering a fine stream of silver liquid into each joint.

"What's that?" Jerry questioned.

"Liquid plastic," Mr. Happy murmured, "like mortar in a brick wall."

Jerry nodded. He glanced down the sloping ramp, then looked up quickly. "No use scaring yourself before it's

time," he said to himself, bending to help Vic with another block.

Twenty minutes later Happy Tom sealed the last joint. "All done?" Vic asked.

Mr. Happy nodded. "Just about. Hand me that machine near your foot."

Jerry picked up a small, compact gadget with a motor in the middle and files on both ends.

With a few skillful strokes Mr. Happy smoothed a rough place here and leveled an overlap there. Then he stepped back. "It's done."

Jerry grinned. "Boy, this is the greatest! Ow . . . my back! I'm going to be stiff for a week."

"Now we'll take the framework down," Mr. Happy announced, as he packed his tools away in a small box and stepped aboard the tiny elevator. "Let's go down."

Once on the ground, Jerry was given the job of building a guard fence of twine and wooden stakes around the base of the completed ramp, as Vic and Mr. Happy dismantled the framework.

Jerry was tying the last length of twine when Vic gave a whoop. "Man oh man, have a look, Jerry!"

Jerry straightened with effort and limped to the truck. He found his Visiospecs and slipped them on.

The ramp, freed from its web of pipes, swept upward into the night sky, a vast arc of turquoise sheen. At the crest it curved, as if in hesitation, then fell earthward in a breath-taking swoop. Still-wet joints flashed like silver lines to add a glint of hardness to the shimmering curtain of blue-green.

107

"Boy oh boy, it's beautiful and . . ." Jerry gasped ". . . high!"

"High is right, spaceman," Vic echoed. "Boy, I can hardly wait until tomorrow!"

Jerry took another long look, then slipped off the goggles. "Mr. Happy, what time . . ."

". . . about two o'clock," the tall man answered, without waiting for Jerry to finish. "We're on right after the Motorcycle Masquerade. You and Vic better be here about one. I'll meet you at the tunnel."

"One o'clock." Jerry glanced at the big clock above the grandstand. "It's only nine now. Gosh, I thought it was three in the morning." He pressed his hand to the small of his back. "Feels like I have been working for two days."

"I'm going to stay here tonight," Mr. Happy explained. "I want to keep an eye on the ramp. Do you want me to drive you home in the truck?"

Vic snickered. "We'd better walk. I don't think Mr. Campbell could stand another sight of your 'empty' truck."

Jerry laughed. "You're probably right, all-star. Let's blast. I'm going to need the sleep."

"Check!"

At the entrance tunnel Jerry turned to wave. However, the tall, sad scientist was standing with his back turned, hands on hips, staring into the night sky where the graceful crest of the ramp would be. "You know, Vic," Jerry whispered, "old 'Honest Abe' doesn't talk much, but I'll bet he's as excited as we are. After all, this means a lot to him."

108

"That's right," Vic agreed. "Hey, I just thought of something."

"No kidding; all by yourself?"

"O.K., funny man," Vic threw a playful punch, "but if we want to get back in here tomorrow we'd better get a pass or something."

"Right you are, old buddy. Let's ask 'Smiley' Campbell. There he is."

The old guard, who had been watching them from the door of his little shack, stepped inside quickly. Vic knocked at the window. "Mr. Campbell, can we talk to you?"

The window raised an eighth of an inch. "Whatcha-want?"

"We'd like to get a pass so we can get back in tomorrow."

The window slammed shut. Vic shrugged and knocked again. "Say, Mr. Campbell, all we want . . ."

The window cracked open and two slips of paper shot out. "There! Go away!"

Jerry scooped up the papers. "Look, all-star, passes for the whole week. We can get in any time we want!"

Vic grinned as he rapped on the window once again. "Thank you very much, Mr. Campbell."

"Go 'way!"

Just then a truck driver, who had been waiting at the gate entrance, leaned out his window. "Hey, what's the holdup?" He punctuated his question with a blast of his horn. The drivers behind him took up the chorus.

"Vic," Jerry shouted above the din, "let's blast!"

"Check! We can short-cut through Elm Street."

Jerry was puffing as they reached the dimly lit street. "Hey, all-star, slow down. This pace is killing me!" He brought out his Jet Cadet Rocket Flash. At best, it helped them miss the largest of the many chuckholes in the little-used street. "With these passes we'll be able to see all the shows. That is," Jerry added, "if we live through tomorrow."

Vic chuckled. "The ramp is as solid as the Golden Gate Bridge, spaceman, and we've been practicing for a week. It ought to be a breeze."

"I guess you're right. At least so far nothing . . ." The quietness behind him was suddenly filled with noise. Jerry twirled.

Vic's frantic cry pushed past the roar. "Jump! Jump!"

Jerry strained, but fear seemed to clamp his feet to the ground. He thrust his hands before him as if this would stop the earsplitting roar. The feeble light of his Rocket Flash poked into the black wall of noise. Suddenly the end of the beam shattered into a cluster of jiggling highlights. Jerry saw the helmet and the goggles and the snarling mouth. "Buck!" he gasped. His fear-locked legs broke free. He dropped the flashlight and dived sideways. The whole world was one deafening explosion. Jerry doubled into a ball as the rasping exhaust blasted white-hot against his legs. Dirt and gravel filled the air as the rocking, roaring motorcycle flashed past. As suddenly as it had torn through the silence of the night, the ugly rasp of the motor faded.

110

Jerry lay gasping. He spat dirt and weeds from his mouth. "Vic, you . . . O.K.?"

"I'm all right," Vic stammered, threshing in the weeds. "Man o-oh-m-man, that guy is out for blood!"

Jerry sat up and took several deep breaths. "What a deal! What a deal!"

"What's that clicking noise?"

Jerry tried to listen above the pounding of his heart. Finally he heard the faint clicking. Then he laughed.

"What's so funny?"

"It's my trusty Jet Cadet Rocket Flash. That's what Buck was aiming at. See out there in the road? If I hadn't dropped it *I* would be lying out there now!"

"But what's the clicking noise?"

111

"The built-in Geiger counter. It hasn't worked since last Christmas. I guess the shock was too much."

Vic stepped to the middle of the road and picked up the noisy flashlight. "Another close shave like this and I'll start clicking."

"Turn it off. Buck might make another try." Jerry struggled to his feet and brushed the weeds out of his hair. "Let's follow Coach Moore's advice about running off pregame jitters, all-star. And this is one time when you won't have to worry about my not keeping up. I'm going to run every step!"

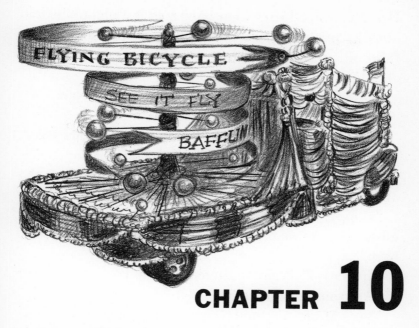

CHAPTER 10

Jerry picked up the jangling phone. " 'Lo," he mumbled, swallowing the last of a cinnamon roll.

"Jet Cadet Lathrop reporting."

"You're coming in loud and clear. Over."

"Now hear this. Since 'Kind Heart' Campbell gave us two official any time passes, let's blast for the fairgrounds early."

"Roger. Why don't you hop into your superlunar space sled and rocket over here?"

"Roger and out."

Jerry cradled the receiver and walked back to the kitchen.

Peggy giggled, "How's your stomach?"

Jerry selected another roll. "Oh, I feel fine, just fine."

He took a bite. "After what happened last night," he told himself, "nothing could scare me." He was finishing his third roll when the doorbell rang. "I'll get it . . . probably Vic."

"Hi," Peggy smiled, as Vic walked into the room.

"Hi, Peggy. Hello, Mr. and Mrs. Barnes."

"All ready for your big ride, Vic?" Jerry's mother asked.

"As ready as I'll ever be, Mrs. Barnes."

Peggy beamed. "I hope you and Jerry and that Mr. What's-his-name are a big success today."

"Happy," Jerry interrupted, "Mr. Happy. Let's blast, all-star, before we break our arms patting ourselves on the back."

"Honestly!" Peggy sputtered.

"Are you going already?"

"Yes, Mom. Vic and I have some official any time passes. . . ."

"We got them last night," Vic began. "Just about didn't have a chance to use them, though. Did Jerry tell. . . ."

"See you at the fairgrounds," Jerry broke in, as he pushed Vic out the door. " 'Bye!"

Vic nearly stumbled down the back steps. "Hey, what's the idea of shoving me?"

Jerry waited until they were in the alley. "All morning I've been trying hard *not* to talk about what happened last night. If my mother found out about Buck's little visit she might worry *me* out of riding the triple decker."

Vic nodded. "Let's cut through town."

The fair was a county-wide attraction, and part of the fun for the farming people was a morning of gossiping

114

and shopping. Saulito's sidewalks were thronged and the streets jammed with cars and trucks.

They pushed their way through the crowd. "What a mob," Jerry murmured.

"The more the merrier," Vic laughed. Then he pointed, "Hey, look!"

Jerry whistled when he saw the huge sign.

WELCOME TO THE SAULITO COUNTY FAIR

Don't miss these stellar opening day attractions!

1:00 SEE! Amazing MOTORCYCLE MAS-QUERADE! 50 riders! Mass formation! Daredevil thrills!

2:00 SEE! Fabulous TRIPLE DECKER FLYING BICYCLE with technicolor smoke screen! One time only!

3:00 SEE! Famous R O Y ''D A K O T A'' JONES, TV Cowboy star and his world-famous trick horse GOLD-EN BOY!

SEE! PARADES HARNESS RAC-ING FIREWORKS BANDS

Jerry whistled again. "Great gyrating gyroscopes, all-star, we're right up there with Dakota Jones!"

"Not to mention his trick horse Golden Boy," Vic added.

"Hey, Jerry, Vic!" Jimmy Taylor came pedaling across the street. "Really something, isn't it?"

115

Jerry glanced up at the sign. "You said it, Jimmy."

"I don't mean the sign," Jimmy blurted. "I mean the truck with all the satellites!"

"Truck? Satellites?"

"Look for yourself!"

Jerry spotted what appeared to be a misplaced parade float working its way slowly through the traffic. It was Happy Tom's rented truck, all but buried beneath a blanket of colorful crepe paper. But, most important, on the back of the truck, whirling around a paper-festooned pole, were at least twenty bright metal balls. Around they streaked, each at its own level and each, it seemed, equipped with a different whistle. The sound was unearthly, a throbbing warble like a thousand distant sirens. Streaks of yellow, blue, green and red arced through the air as each spinning satellite trailed a brightly colored banner. "THE FABULOUS TRIPLE DECKER FLYING BICYCLE," the biggest proclaimed; others announced: "SEE IT FLY *TODAY*—SAULITO COUNTY FAIR," "Mysterious! Baffling! Breath taking!" "See it Today!"

"Hey," Jerry shouted, "look who's driving! Hi, Mr. Happy!"

The scientist waved. "Want a ride?"

Jerry opened the door. "Sure thing! Come on, Vic."

Vic crowded in the middle. "I'll bet this was the surprise you mentioned yesterday."

Happy Tom nodded.

"Surprise is right!" Jerry laughed. "Boy, what a keen idea!"

116

"It was your idea," Vic chided. "Talk about breaking your arm patting your own back. But, no lie, this does look great. If this doesn't bring the people, nothing will."

Mr. Happy threaded the glittering, warbling truck through the crowded street. All along the way, people gathered to point and stare. Several of Jerry and Vic's friends waved from the sidewalk. Bob Graham puffed alongside on his bike for a block or so. At the main gate Happy Tom stilled the whirling satellites.

Mr. Campbell, extra busy, drew back his clipboard to deliver his usual slap as the truck lumbered through the gate. At the last moment he spotted Jerry and Vic, checked his swing, mumbled something and stumbled backward into his shack.

Happy Tom followed a route which had been roped off from the milling crowd.

"Looks like everyone in the whole state is here!" Jerry breathed. He leaned out the window. The sharp smell of hot dogs and popcorn blended with the sugar-sweet scent of cotton candy. Fun rides, going full blast, rattled and clanked beyond the stock barns, giving a mechanical background to the animal grunts and bleats.

Suddenly Mr. Happy jammed on the brakes. Both Jerry and Vic piled forward against the dashboard.

Jerry rubbed his forehead. "What's the matter?"

Tall Happy Tom seemed to be listening. He reached into his shirt pocket and brought out a tiny square box. There was the sound of glass breaking and heavy thumps. Jerry ducked instinctively. The sounds, however, were coming from the little box Happy Tom was holding.

117

"Radio," Mr. Happy murmured, answering an unasked question. "Someone is breaking into my shack." His words were punctuated by heavy thuds and the crunch of shattering wood.

"You two hop out and check the triple decker!" Mr. Happy snapped. "It's parked beneath the grandstand in the tunnel entrance! Hurry!" He was already swinging the truck around.

Jerry shoved at the door. "Sure you don't want us to come along?"

Happy Tom shook his head. "Bike is more important! Quickly!"

Jerry watched the gaily bedecked truck roll away. "Gee, I hope nothing happens."

"Let's see if we can find the triple decker, spaceman."

The guard at the tunnel entrance, who had greeted them last night by falling flat on his back, now eyed them suspiciously.

"We're . . . er . . . we're going to ride the flying bicycle," Jerry explained.

The guard shook his head. "Can't get in without a pass."

Jerry caught Vic's wink. "Are you any relation to Mr. Campbell at the main gate?" Vic asked.

"Brothers!" the man snapped.

"That figures," Vic muttered.

"What say?"

"I said . . . er . . . bigger. He's a little bigger."

Jerry fished into his pocket. "Here's my pass."

The man snatched the paper, then thrust it back. He seemed disappointed. "O.K., bike's in that room."

Vic showed his pass, then followed.

"Looks just fine," Jerry grinned, as he pulled back the canvas cover.

"Hummm." Vic narrowed his eyes. "You don't suppose old 'Honest Abe' was just trying to get rid of us?"

"Could be. Anyone who would make all that noise just breaking into a dinky shack might be real dangerous. Or maybe he heard something on that dandy little 'matchbox' radio that we missed."

Vic shrugged, "Well, there's nothing we can do about

it now." He pulled back the canvas cover. "Let's have a look around; maybe I can win a prize or two."

Jerry smiled to himself as they pushed their way through the crowd in the sawdust-strewn carnival area. Vic was expert when it came to popping balloons with darts or throwing rings or basketballs, but when it came to knocking wooden milk bottles over with a baseball, he was deadly. Last year he won seventeen giant stuffed pandas and twenty-six skull-shaped ash trays with simulated ruby eyes in a matter of minutes.

The eyes of the heavy-jowled operator of the baseball-throwing booth widened. "Oh, no, not you again!"

Vic grinned and dug some coins from his pocket.

The man held up his hands. "Please," he pleaded, "let's not go through this again. Tell you what—I'll give both you and your buddy one of these brand-new stuffed tigers with genuine agate eyes. And," he added, when Vic seemed to hesitate, "a free pass to all the rides! How about that?"

"That's fine with me," Vic laughed. "Thank you very much."

Jerry giggled as they walked away. "Next year he might give you the whole booth!"

"I hope not! I had a heck of a time getting rid of those stuffed pandas last year! Here, take your pass."

"Thanks, muscles. Let's ride the Space Spinner first."

The Space Spinner, a sort of combination Ferris Wheel and Octopus, was easy to find. It towered nearly sixty feet in the air. In a matter of minutes Jerry was leaning over the side of a swinging gondola. He nudged Vic. "Look

120

over there—you can see the row of stakes around the ramp."

A sudden glint of light flashed in the distance. "What was that?" Vic gasped.

"Gosh, I don't know!" Jerry craned his neck as the Space Spinner dipped earthward. Halfway down he heard a dull thud like a thump on some giant oil drum. "Listen!" They climbed again.

"Look!" Vic was pointing. "Smoke!"

An ugly twist of black smoke was rising over the spot where the flash had appeared. As Jerry stared, two more flashes glinted in quick succession. He began to count under his breath, "One thousand one, one thousand two. . . ."

"Listen!" Vic exclaimed. "Fire engines!"

Over the wail of sirens came twin thuds. ". . . one thousand six," Jerry counted aloud.

"Huh?"

Jerry was busy adjusting his glasses. "How far is Happy Tom's shack from here?"

"About a mile. . . ." Vic stared at the yellow curtain forming beneath the black smoke. "Oh, my gosh!"

Jerry nodded. "I counted the seconds between flash and sound. It came out to a mile, all-star."

"If that smoke isn't coming from Happy Tom's shack, it's coming from something right next door!"

Jerry nodded grimly. "And Happy Tom hasn't a neighbor within half a mile."

The Space Spinner ground to a halt. Jerry was first out. "You can see the smoke from the ground now!"

121

"Let's head back to the grandstand," Vic suggested. "I think we'd better have another look at the triple decker."

"Check! Gosh, I hope we're wrong. I hope it isn't Mr. Happy's shack at all! Probably 'Honest Abe' will be waiting for us when we get there."

The tunnel was deserted, save for the sour-faced guard.

Vic tugged at the striped canvas. "Good as gold! At least the triple decker is safe. Let's put these stuffed tigers in the framework here."

"O.K., then we can push it out and watch the motorcycle show while we're waiting for Mr. Happy."

The Silver Piston Motorcycle Club was a well-organized group, Jerry decided. In the bustle of last minute preparations each member had a particular job: Costumes were adjusted, touches of make-up were added and the final polish applied to already-gleaming chrome on the handsomely decorated machines.

Shorty, decked out as an Indian in full-feathered headdress, waved from the distance. Three buffaloes were busy combing each other's tails. One of the shaggy beasts turned out to be Skinhead.

Then, amid a roll of drums from the bandstand, a voice boomed: "Good afternoon, ladies and gentlemen. Welcome to the thirty-fifth annual Saulito County Fair! Now, let the show begin!"

To the surge of a military march, a parade of paper-ribboned cars circled slowly into view. Jerry recognized the Mayor of Saulito riding in the lead car.

"There's Chief Pinkerton, your old buddy," Vic chided, pointing to a car third in line.

122

Jerry grinned, then stopped grinning as Policeman Woods came hurrying out onto the track. He must have had something important to whisper because the huge police chief bounced out of the car and lumbered away.

The parade rolled to a stop in front of the grandstand and the dignitaries trooped onto a flag-draped platform. The Mayor told everyone how Saulito was growing. Another man talked about farming, and finally it was one o'clock.

The Motorcycle Masquerade roared to life. Costumed cyclists depicted a wagon train under Indian attack. More cyclists joined, dressed as cavalry soldiers. A pitch battle followed with breath-taking stunts and some very funny comedy antics.

Shorty, playing the part of an eager, but dumb, Indian, blundered into the center of the circled wagons. Jerry bent double from laughter as Shorty skidded about haplessly in the midst of the enraged "pioneers."

When Jerry straightened he found himself face to face with the fussy Director of Special Events, C. H. Twilliger. The tall, thin man looked even more confused than he had when Vic spilled the purple smoke bomb all over his desk. His eyebrows were twitching a mile a minute. His mouth was working, too, but Jerry couldn't hear above the snarl and blat of the motorcycles.

The tall man pointed wildly. ". . . telephone. . . ."

Jerry turned. He couldn't see any telephones. Mr. Twilliger frantically gestured toward a small room in the tunnel entrance. They all crowded in and the slender man slammed the door against the roar.

123

"Oh, this is dreadful! Now, let me see, it's exactly one-thirty-three!" He brought out a spotless white handkerchief and began dabbing his forehead. "Oh, dear, what am I going to do?"

"What are you going to do about what?"

"What's the matter, Mr. Gilliger?"

Mr. Twilliger cleared his throat. "At exactly one-eighteen Mr. Happy telephoned me . . . he's in the hospital!"

CHAPTER 11

"The hospital!" Jerry and Vic shouted in unison.

Mr. Twilliger fluttered his fingers. "Let me finish! Mr. Happy phoned from the hospital and told me to tell you that his shack had been blown up . . . completely destroyed!"

"Shack blown up!" Jerry screeched. "Mr. Happy in the hospital!"

"What's he doing in the hospital?" Vic echoed.

Mr. Twilliger dabbed his forehead with a white handkerchief. "Oh, dear! Oh, dear! Let's see now, it's exactly one-forty-one. . . ."

"But what happened to Mr. Happy?" Jerry demanded.

"Mr. Happy? Oh, yes! He burnt his hands rescuing some sort of formula. This is dreadful . . . dreadful!"

"Is he badly hurt?"

Vic broke in. "He can't be hurt too badly if he was able to talk on the phone, spaceman."

"Yes! I mean no, he's not badly hurt . . . but . . . but . . . oh, this is dreadful!"

"But what?"

"He won't be able to ride on the triple decker! Oh, dear, what am I going to do? It's exactly one-forty-two!"

"Vic and I can still operate the bike, Mr. Hilliger."

Mr. Twilliger's eyes widened. "A *triple decker* bicycle with only *two* riders would be . . . dishonest! No! No!" He stamped his white shoe. "I'll just have to cancel the whole thing!"

"Don't do that," Jerry interrupted. "All we have to do is find someone to ride in Mr. Happy's place!"

"Sure!" Vic agreed.

"Let's see," Jerry adjusted his glasses, "who could we get? Maybe Chief Pinkerton."

"Chief Pinkerton!" Vic gasped. "Are you nuts?"

"It was just a thought, all-star."

"Dreadful, simply dreadful! I knew this flying contraption was a mistake the first time I saw it. Oh, dear, it's exactly one-forty-nine!"

"Hey, Mr. Gilliham," Jerry shouted, "I know who can take Mr. Happy's place! You!"

"Mr. Gilliham . . . who's Mr. Gill . . . ME!" Mr. Twilliger looked as if he had been hit with a bucket of mud. "On a flying bicycle? Oh, my goodness!"

"Sure," Vic laughed, "there's nothing to it. You won't have a thing to do except enjoy the view."

"It's one-fifty-two! Oh, my, what a dreadful thing . . . ride a flying bicycle! I'm going to call Mr. Happy." Mr. Twilliger twirled, pulled open the door and was gone.

Jerry turned to Vic. "Gosh, I hope Happy Tom is O.K."

"So do I. One guess on who did the exploding, space-man."

"Buck!"

Vic nodded as they stepped through the door.

The motorized Indians had given way to formations of goblins, witches and demons as the cyclists roared through "A Halloween Night."

"Hey, Jerry," Vic called, "give me a hand with these smoke bombs."

Jerry knelt and began sorting the cans. "That's funny," he muttered, glancing toward the cyclists.

"Huh, what's funny?"

"Do you remember Buck's motorcycle? It was all covered with gadgets, like Happy Tom's bike."

"So?"

"I could have sworn I just saw it out there. Look, that guy with the devil's costume!" Jerry pointed as the line of weaving cycles parted. Sunlight glittered on an ornate motorcycle and shimmered over the rider's blood-red mask. Then the line closed.

Vic frowned. "I see what you mean, but Skinhead said that Buck didn't join the Silver Pistons."

"Now, let me see . . ." It was the voice of Mr. Twilliger. He was carrying a paper-wrapped bundle. ". . . it's exactly one-fifty-eight. Oh, my goodness! Oh, dear . . ."

"Did you talk to Mr. Happy?"

"Is he all right?"

"Yes! Yes! Now, then, here are the costumes he ordered." He began tearing at the paper.

"Costumes?" Jerry quizzed.

"This is yours," Mr. Twilliger stuffed a coat into Jerry's arms, "and yours," he thrust another at Vic, "and this one was Mr. Happy's." The slender man wiggled into the coat. Like the others, it was made of scarlet satin material with huge brass buttons. Fancy braid covered the front and gawdy, jewel-studded epaulets perched on each shoulder. "Oh, dear, it's much too large!"

Vic held out his arms. "Hey, get a load of me!"

Jerry snorted. "The greatest, all-star! You look like Captain Space on TV."

At that moment the entire troop of motorcyclists roared before the grandstand in a final mass formation. The huge crowd thundered its approval for a fine show. The band struck up a spirited tune.

"Ladiesssandgentlemennn," a voice announced, "the Saulito County Fair now presents a scientific marvel—demonstrated for the first time in history! The one . . . the only . . . the fabulous . . . triple decker FLYING bicycle . . . with a technicolor smoke screen! Here they are, folks. Let's give them a big hand!"

The band blared forth with a triumphant fanfare as Mr. Twilliger, Jerry and Vic strutted forward. Suddenly Jerry and Vic scuttled back into the tunnel. The band faltered, then took up the fanfare again.

"Good heavens!" Mr. Twilliger hissed. "Where did you go?"

128

"We forgot the bicycle," Jerry giggled.

"Oh, dear! Oh, my goodness! Dreadful! It's exactly two-three!"

"Jerry!" There was alarm in Vic's sudden whisper. "Look! Near the tunnel! The guy in the red mask . . . he didn't leave with the others!"

Jerry forgot about the thousands of cheering people in the grandstand as he focused on one figure hunched over a glittering, gadget-cluttered motorcycle.

The man reached up to tear away his mask. Piggish eyes glinted above an ugly, snarl-twisted mouth.

Jerry stiffened. "Vic, it *is* Buck!"

The announcer's voice drowned Vic's startled reply. "In a moment these three brave riders will defy the law of gravity itself! They will soar into the air. . . ."

For the first time since Buck had come roaring at him from the darkness on Elm Street, Jerry felt his heart pound. "What is this character up to now?" he asked himself. He was certain Buck had blown up Mr. Happy's shack. Now the man, his mind twisted with revenge, was poised like a giant vulture not thirty yards away. But why? Then Jerry answered his own question. "Vic, he's going to ram us!"

Vic's eyes widened. "My gosh, I think you're right! We'll be sitting ducks!"

Meanwhile Mr. Twilliger had quit fussing and was acting the part of a brave bicycle rider. "Look sharp there," he hissed, "it's exactly two-six."

Jerry winced. "At least he's enjoying himself."

". . . a mystery of the age," the announcer continued.

129

"You'll be amazed, mystified, astounded, puzzled . . ."

". . . and flattened like a day-old pancake," Jerry added.

"Now, let's see . . ." Mr. Twilliger whispered, "how . . . er . . . how do I get on this thing?"

"Just climb up, Mr. Billiker," Jerry directed. "We'll hold the bike."

Mr. Twilliger scrambled up the wobbling framework and settled himself on the top deck.

"O.K., Jerry," Vic whispered, "up you go. Hand Mr. What's-his-name this smoke bomb."

Jerry boosted himself onto the seat. "Here, Mr. Billingham, grab this smoke bomb. Shake it when we tell you. All set, Vic? Let's blast!"

Vic pushed off. The triple decker wobbled as Mr. Twilliger shifted nervously.

"Sit still!" Jerry snapped.

The band struck up a spirited version of "Bicycle Built for Two" as they passed in front of the grandstand.

Jerry glanced toward the ramp and nearly fell off his seat. "Vic!" he gulped. "VIC, THE RAMP! We left the Visiospecs in the truck! We can't see the ramp!"

"Oh, my gosh!"

Jerry strained his eyes trying to make out the furrow of matted grass at the base of the ramp. By now all the grass between the stakes had been trampled flat. "Vic, can you see anything?"

"Not a thing . . . and we've got to hit it dead center!"

"Well, now, this isn't as bad as I thought," Mr. Twilliger called from above, well out of earshot. He waved

130

jauntily. "Perhaps we should pass in front of the grandstand again. It's exactly two-ten."

"You're a big help," Jerry muttered under his breath. "But it would give us a little more time. Hey, Vic, let's take another turn in front of the stand." He shook his smoke bomb into operation. "Let's start the smoke screen."

Before the triple decker had covered another twenty feet, a huge cloud of multiclored smoke billowed behind. They leaned around a turn and doubled back.

"Yes, yes!" Mr. Twilliger puffed. "I always knew this would be an excellent show . . . a credit to the Special Events Department. Oops! Say there . . . er . . . Barnes . . . you dropped your smoke bomb."

"By golly, you're right," Jerry agreed. "It just slipped out of my hand." He watched the bouncing can. "Vic, I threw the bomb on purpose. . . ."

Vic was not watching the can, however. He was staring toward the tunnel where Buck was stomping the starting lever of his cycle.

Jerry stared after him. Despite Buck's frantic kicks, the motor only coughed. "How lucky can we be?" Jerry whistled, as they rolled past.

The huge audience broke into applause. The announcer, evidently realizing that the triple decker wasn't going to fly this trip, stammered into a description of the smoke screen. "The . . . er . . . technicolor smoke screen, ladieessandgentlemennn . . . a . . . a . . . display of chemistry magic!"

"Splendid!" Mr. Twilliger shouted. "Just as I thought all along!"

Once again they brought the triple decker about, only to glide into a thick fog.

"Spaceman, I can't see a thing!"

Jerry peered through the swirling cloud. "Just keep pumping, old buddy, I'll guide. Man oh man, I didn't think the smoke would be this thick!"

Sailing above the layer of smoke, Mr. Twilliger waved and bowed as they swept past the stand.

"What's Buck doing?" Vic hissed.

"Still trying to get his motor started. This is our lucky day . . ." Just then the powerful motorcycle roared into life. "We've had it now, spaceman!"

Jerry edged the speeding triple decker closer to the row of stakes until he spotted his smoke bomb. It was standing on edge, balanced, so it would seem, in mid-air. "Good deal!"

"What?"

"I know where the ramp is, Vic. I dropped my smoke bomb accidentally on purpose. It's leaning against the side of the ramp."

"Come about, there!" Mr. Twilliger ordered from above. He was sitting ramrod straight, looking for all the world like an admiral on his flagship.

"Aye aye, sir," Jerry muttered. "How you doing, Vic?"

"O.K., spaceman," Vic puffed. "But if we miss the ramp I'm going to be too pooped to make another run. Can you see Buck?"

Jerry craned his neck. "No, but I can hear him. If we miss the ramp you won't have to worry about being pooped, old buddy." Jerry caught sight of his tilted smoke bomb. "Here we go!"

Even the snarl of Buck's motorcycle was muffled in the quiet that settled over the vast stadium. Everyone seemed to be holding his breath. Even Admiral Twilliger, bending forward now and gripping the handle bars with whitened knuckles, was speechless.

The loudest noise Jerry could hear was the thumpity-thump of his own heart. He took a deep breath and pointed the bouncing triple decker at a spot to the left of his smoke bomb. He fought to keep the awkward contraption in line.

Vic hunched and pumped powerfully, straining with all his might. The triple decker gathered speed. The grass of the arena became a blur; a greenish torrent that flashed beneath them, tugging and yanking at the bicycle's wheels.

Jerry clamped the handle grips so hard his fingers ached. It seemed that the bouncing, lunging triple decker wanted to veer in every direction but straight. Acid, searing smoke coiled and lashed across his eyes. For an instant he was blinded. He squinted through tears, panic gripping his chest. "I've lost it . . . I've lost the ramp!"

Then, with a gentle jolt, the triple decker tilted and began to climb. Up and up they rolled, toward the dazzling sun. Jerry remembered the confetti box. A geyser of fluttering color bits erupted above them as they cleared the smoke. Ten, twenty, thirty feet they sailed into the air. Jerry triggered the balloon launcher. A huge cluster of silver and gold balloons blossomed into the sky, dancing and glittering.

133

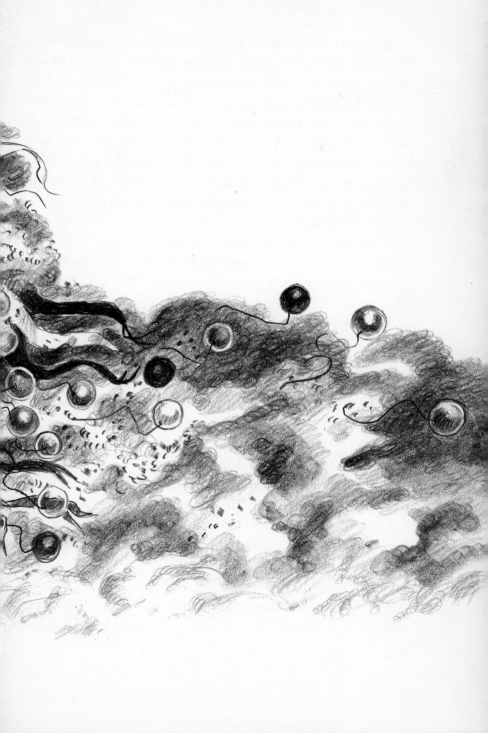

Jerry saw Buck rocket through smoke and confetti and flash onto the arena grass directly beneath them. For an instant a twisted grin smeared across his ugly face. His timing was perfect, but the smile became a wild cry as man and machine slammed against invisible bricks, instead of the triple decker. The cycle, minus rider, fenders and several dozen ornaments, came flying out the other side. It bounced in great crunching cart wheels. The ramp shuddered from the impact, lurching and swaying like a wounded elephant.

"I've lost the pedals!" Vic gasped.

Jerry struggled to keep his balance, but a foot shy of the crest the triple decker teetered to a stop. "Get off! Let the bike fall!"

"No! No!" Mr. Twilliger yelled. "The show must go on . . ."

"Get down!" Jerry shouted, as he dropped beside Vic. Together they struggled to keep the triple decker upright. Mr. Twilliger came scrambling down amid a torrent of confetti. "What am I standing on? Nothing! There's nothing here!" His words were lost under a grinding rumble.

"What's happening?" Vic stammered.

"It's crumbling!" Jerry hissed. "The ramp is crumbling like that block out at the shack. It's crumbling to dust!"

Even as he spoke, a section of the ramp under them gave way with a crunch. The triple decker nosed into the invisible crevice.

"Let's get off this thing!" Vic gasped.

Jerry dropped to his hands and knees. The next few seconds were a blur of clawing and clutching, as he scram-

136

bled from one invisible block to another. There was the sound of a siren and a brilliant flash from somewhere behind him. His feet touched solid earth. He staggered backward. Vic dropped to the ground before him. Mr. Twilliger and the triple decker came to earth in a series of jerks. Through the smoke Jerry could make out another figure; it was Police Chief Pinkerton bending over Buck.

"It's him, all right!" the huge chief bellowed.

Jerry stared dizzily as a second policeman came into view. Together they dragged the limp Buck to his feet and faded from sight. Vic reappeared, pushing the triple decker. "You O.K.?"

"I guess so," Jerry stammered, shaking his head. "Where's Mr. Twarthingham?"

Just then the tall Director of Special Events staggered past. "Let's see now . . ." He was flipping through a little white notebook which he was holding upside down. ". . . it's exactly thirty-four past fifty-two. After the technicolored smoke cycle comes Cowboy Jim and his golden pig. No, no! . . . his golden calf . . . cow . . ."

"Let's blast," Jerry muttered, grabbing the triple decker.

They pushed their way through the thinning smoke and into the tunnel entrance. The only sound in the vast grandstand was the whisper of a breeze and the soft flutter of the colorful confetti.

"Just listen to that applause," Jerry groaned, as they slouched toward the main gate. "If silence was golden, we'd be millionaires, old buddy!"

CHAPTER 12

"The fabulous triple decker flying flop," Jerry snorted, "complete with technicolor nothing! Happy Tom in the hospital . . . his shack blown to smithereens . . . the transoplastic ramp nothing but a pile of dust! Man oh man, we couldn't have loused this deal up better if we tried!"

Vic shrugged. "We still have the triple decker."

"Fat lot of good that does! As soon as we tell Happy Tom the dandy news let's ride over to my garage and take it apart."

"Check," Vic agreed, as they turned into the hospital driveway.

Jerry was the first through the big glass entrance. White uniformed nurses bustled noiselessly about. A voice was calling quietly: "Dr. Johnson . . . Dr. Johnson . . . Please report to Ward B."

A woman dressed in a pink uniform smiled from behind a desk. "May I help you?"

"We're looking for Mr. Happy."

"He burned himself this morning," Vic offered.

The woman nodded. "That would probably be in Emergency." She stood. "Wait here for a moment. I'll see if I can locate him. Happy, did you say?"

Jerry nodded.

"Wonder why she doesn't wear a white uniform like the other nurses?" Vic quizzed.

"She's not a nurse, all-star, she's a Pink Lady. They help out in the hospital for free. My mother was one last summer. I wonder what Happy Tom will have to say when we tell him the good news."

"One thing for sure, spaceman, Happy Tom isn't going to be happy!"

Just then the Pink Lady returned. She sat down and picked up her telephone. "Mr. Happy was in the Emergency Ward earlier this afternoon," she explained. "One of our house doctors was in attendance. I'll see if I can get him. Hello, Operator?" The woman glanced up from a sheet of paper she had brought with her. "Oh, never mind, Operator." She replaced the receiver. "Dr. Lustig."

A stocky, white-robed young man strode to the desk.

"These boys want to talk to a Mr. Thomas Happy, Doctor. I believe he was in Emergency this morning."

The young doctor took the paper. "Happy? Oh, yes, a tall, sad-looking fellow . . ."

140

"That's him, Doctor," Jerry interrupted.

"Is he badly hurt?" Vic asked.

"Can we talk to him?"

"One at a time," the doctor chuckled. "No, he wasn't badly hurt. Yes, you can talk to him. Of course, he's not here in the hospital."

"He's not here?"

"He had no reason to stay; the injuries were minor." The doctor glanced at the paper. "Didn't give any home address."

"No wonder," Jerry smiled grimly, "someone blew up his sha . . . home." Then he shrugged, "Well, thank you very much, Doctor."

"And you, too, ma'am," Vic added.

Outside, Jerry smacked his fist into his palm. "What a deal! Now we can't even find Mr. Happy. This has turned out to be the biggest flop in history!" Then he snapped his fingers. "Hey, I'll bet I know where he went . . . out to his lab!"

"Sure! Let's ride out there now!"

"Check! But let's take off these jazzy coats, all-star. I'm beginning to feel like a drum major!"

A pall of yellowish smoke, three charred posts and a twisted metal pipe was all that remained of Mr. Happy's shack. But as they turned into the driveway past the clump of bushes, Jerry saw the real damage. "Vic!" he gasped. "The lab! The storage room! Oh, my gosh!"

They parked the triple decker next to Captain Towne's bright red car and sprinted to the edge of a mammoth crater. Through a curtain of dirty yellow, Jerry could see

141

the crushed bits of what had been Happy Tom's lab. Burnt shreds of cloth and a few splinters marked the grave of his beautiful underground apartment. The storage room was now a huge trench floored with a few fragments of cement.

"Look at that," Jerry groaned. "You wouldn't know anything had ever been there. Everything's gone . . . the shack, the lab, the . . ."

"Please don't stand too near the edge, boys." It was the voice of Fire Captain Towne. "Might cave in at any moment."

Jerry retreated a few steps. "Have you seen a tall, sort of sad-faced man around here?"

The mild-mannered fire captain shook his head. "Haven't seen a soul, except Chief Pinkerton. My, look at the size of that hole. The chief mentioned something about deliberate dynamiting. Whoever did it must have used an armful of explosives . . . and for just that little shack!"

"Probably one of those guys who enjoys his work."

"Ho, ho!" Captain Towne laughed. "Enjoys his work! That's a good one, Gerald!" He was still chuckling as he climbed into his bright red car. "Drop by and see us, boys . . . visiting hours one to three on Thursdays. And, Gerald, don't forget to call us when you need help . . . keeps us on our toes, you know. Good-by!"

Jerry glanced at Vic as the big fire truck followed the captain's car. "I'll bet 'Honest Abe' found out what happened and took off like a big bird!"

Vic scooped up a rock and bounced it expertly off one of the charred posts. "I wouldn't blame him. No ramp, no lab and now, no Happy Tom . . ."

142

"Come to think of it," Jerry broke in, glancing back into the smoking pit, "no more bicycles. We left the wheels and chains from ours in the lab."

Vic grunted. "Gosh, I'd forgotten all about that." He threw another rock. "Well, you know what they say about keeping a stiff upper lip."

"Sure thing, muscles. That's about all we've got left from this whole deal . . . a big, fat, stiff upper lip! Let's blast for my place."

As they sped through town Jerry heard the faint sound of cheers and shouts from the fairgrounds. He could almost feel the front wheel of the triple decker bumping onto the invisible ramp again. What a sight that must have been. He winced at the thought. "Boy oh boy, Vic, I can hear the guys now. They're really going to kid us about this! 'Thay, you guyth,' " he mimicked chubby Bob Graham, " 'you thure looked crathy jumping around like that! Goth!' "

"He'll be about half right, too," Vic muttered, as they turned into the alley. He brought the triple decker to a skidding halt.

Jerry scampered into his lab and returned with a handful of tools. "Take a good look, all-star," he motioned. "This is your last chance to see the Fabulous Triple Decker Flying Bicycle!"

Later, after Vic had ridden away on Happy Tom's bike, Jerry heard his folks return. He raised his eyes from the model of a rocket he had been halfheartedly assembling and sighed. "At least *they* won't make fun of me. As a matter of fact, they probably won't say anything, except a

143

kind word or two. Right now I don't even feel like kind words."

The tiny rocket was nearly complete when he heard the door open behind him. He turned at the sound of his mother's voice.

"There you are. Dinner is ready."

"I don't feel much like eating, Mom." Jerry scooped up the remaining parts of the rocket. "Think I'll just finish this in my room."

"Still excited from the fair?"

"I feel about as excited," Jerry mumbled, as he slouched up the back steps, "as a spongeful of cement."

His mother started to say something, then seemed to think better of it.

"Hi, Jerry!" Peggy shouted, as he scuffled through the dining room. "Gee, you were . . ."

"I know," Jerry nodded. "Thanks, anyway."

He heard his sister's surprised gasp. "What's the matter with him?"

"Let him go," Mr. Barnes interrupted. "It's been a strain. It was a fine show, son."

"Sure, Dad. Thanks." He dragged himself up the stairs. "That's the nice thing about a family," he added under his breath. "Even when you pull off the world's biggest boo-boo, they stand behind you three hundred per cent."

It wasn't until he slipped between the sheets of his bed that he realized how tired he was. "Dad is right. This day has been a strain." He punched his pillow. "And tomorrow's going to be even worse!"

CHAPTER 13

In the morning Jerry lay motionless for a long while. Then he dragged himself up and dressed slowly. The family was buzzing at the dining room table. Jerry took a deep breath before he walked in.

"Well, how do you feel this morning?" his father asked, glancing over the Sunday paper.

"Fine, I guess," Jerry mumbled. "Hungry mostly."

"I should think so," his mother smiled, bustling in from the kitchen. "You haven't eaten since breakfast yesterday."

Suddenly Peggy burst out in a fit of giggling.

Jerry slouched into his chair. "Aw, cut it out, Peg. You don't have to rub it in."

Peggy swallowed her laughter. "Rub it in? What do you mean?"

Jerry dug into his grapefruit. "All right, I know it was a flop . . ."

"A flop? What?"

"You know very well what! The fabulous flying bicycle, that's what! Come on, Peg . . ."

"A flop! Daddy, show him the newspaper."

Mr. Barnes unfolded the paper and spread it out on the table.

"Look, Jerry!" Peggy squealed. "Look at the headline!"

Jerry leaned forward. Across the top of the front page, in big, black letters, he read: "LOCAL BOYS BIG HIT AT FAIR." And beneath the headline: "Gerald Barnes, Victor Lathrop and C. H. Twilliger astound huge crowd with 'flying bicycle.' "

Mr. Barnes chuckled. "So you thought your bicycle was a failure. Well, believe me, it was a thrilling stunt! Let me read what the paper has to say. He cleared his throat.

"Saulito—July 5. The huge opening day crowd at the Saulito County Fair was thrilled yesterday by two native sons and the fair's own Director of Special Events. Gerald Barnes and Victor Lathrop, together with Clarence H. Twilliger, soared over forty feet into the air, trailing a beautiful technicolor smoke screen. Then the talented trio performed feats of mid-air gymnastics as a motorcycle, driven at top speed, passed directly beneath them. They leaped and cavorted without visible support and finally descended, unaided, in a dramatic finale. The crowd sat in amazed silence for a full minute. The applause that finally followed was the most thunderous ever heard in the County Fair grandstand."

147

His father paused to turn the page. Jerry stuck his elbow into the middle of his forgotten grapefruit.

"A slight accident marred the performance when the motor-cyclist evidently lost his balance and fell. He was apparently not hurt, however, as ever-alert Chief of Police, Volney K. Pinkerton, assisted by Officer Rodney Woods, were seen helping the cyclist from the arena.

Saulitons can be proud of talented Gerald and Victor, as well as the brilliant Director of Special Events, Twilliger, for providing a spectacle that will long be remembered."

"Just think of that!" Peggy burst out. "Jerry's name in headlines!"

"Y-y-yeah," Jerry stammered, wiping grapefruit juice from his elbow, "think of that!" Just then the doorbell rang. "I'll get it."

Vic stood on the front steps, surrounded by a crowd of grinning school friends. There was a funny smile on his face. "Read the paper?"

Jerry nodded. "Just now finished." He stepped outside as Bob Graham crowded forward.

"Thay, you guyth really put on a show! Got your nameth in the newthpaper and everything! How did you make that bithycle fly?"

"Yeah, Jerry," someone else demanded, "Vic wouldn't tell us. How come you could stay up in the air like that?"

Jerry fumbled with his glasses. "Well, we didn't exactly fly . . ."

Just then Mrs. Barnes appeared. "Good morning, boys."

"Good morning, Mrs. Barnes," Vic answered, leading a chorus of greetings.

"Jerry, are you ready for church? We're going to leave now."

"Can Vic come with us?"

"If he wants to. Come along now."

"We'll thee you guyth after church," Bob Graham shouted.

"Will you tell us the secret then?" Jimmy Taylor asked.

"Can we ride the flying bike sometime?"

Jerry waved his hand. "Yeah . . . er . . . see you guys after church, O.K.?" Then he ducked into the house, pushing Vic before him. "Great roaring rockets, all-star, what are we going to do? I sure wish Happy Tom was around. Should we tell them about the ramp?"

"That's just it, spaceman," Vic whispered. "I did and they don't believe me. When I tried to explain about the

149

ramp to my folks, I don't think even they believed me!"

Peggy came fluttering into the hall. "Hi, Vic! How does it feel to be a big star? Let's go, Jerry. Daddy's waiting in the car."

"Come on, big star!" Jerry giggled. "Your car is waiting." He tried to dodge Vic's playful punch.

It seemed to Jerry that three times the usual number of people were going to church that morning and every one of them seemed to be asking questions.

"Jerry has been working for me this summer," Mr. Proctor announced in a loud voice. "Isn't that right, Jerry?" He bent slightly. "You'll tell me, won't you, Jerry?"

"Tell what, Mr. Proctor?"

"How you managed to fly through the air."

Jerry glanced at Vic. "Well, Mr. Proctor, we didn't actually fly. We were riding on a ramp. Mr. Happy made it in his underground lab."

Mr. Proctor straightened and lost his smile. "Ramp? Underground lab?"

"Kidding aside, Gerald," someone questioned, "just how did you manage to get that bicycle to fly?"

"It's the truth!" Jerry exclaimed. "He built this big invisible ramp in his underground lab . . ."

Mr. Proctor shook his head. "Now, Jerry, I personally talked to Twilliger. He didn't mention anything about a ramp. He said he was rolling along the ground and then, just like that, he flew right up into the air. Come on, Gerald, what's the secret? Balloons? Propellers? Mirrors?"

150

"Gosh, Mr. Proctor," Vic broke in, "Mr. Twilliger wouldn't know about anything anyway. It's just like Jerry said . . . we built this big ramp and then rode up on top of it."

Mr. Proctor shrugged. "If that's the case, I'd really like to see it."

"Oh, it sort of crumbled away . . . er . . . the ramp isn't there any more."

"Well," Mr. Proctor pursed his lips, "I'll settle for this underground lab. I'm sure that will be a sight."

Jerry spread his hands. "That's . . . er . . . well, that's gone, too."

"No ramp! No laboratory!" someone exclaimed. "About all that's left is this Mr. Happy!"

Jerry scuffed at a pebble on the ground. "Well . . . er . . . Mr. Happy has sort of gone, too."

"Hummm," the tall hardware store owner mumbled.

Just then Mrs. Barnes joined the group.

"Good morning, Mrs. Barnes." Mr. Proctor doffed his hat. "We were just having an interesting talk with your famous son. But he and Victor are acting very mysterious about this whole thing."

Jerry glanced at Vic. "It's about time to go inside, isn't it? Is it all right if Vic and I walk home after Sunday school, Mom?"

His mother nodded.

As they crowded into the church basement, Jerry murmured, "I see what you mean, Vic. First the kids and now even the grownups . . . nobody believes us when we tell them about the ramp or anything."

151

The Sunday school teacher talked about honesty. Jerry found himself puzzling over what happened when you spoke the truth and it sounded like you were just trying to hide something. It was hard to figure.

Sunday school over, he and Vic skipped out a rear exit and ducked through a back alley.

"Boy oh boy," Vic muttered, "if I have to answer one more question I'll flip my lid!"

"You can say that again, all-star; especially when nobody believes what you say!"

Vic scooped up a tin can and began to "dribble" it down an imaginary basketball floor. He was about to lay it in for a game-winning score when he stopped dead. "Oh, no!"

Jerry glanced up the street. The shiny black-and-white squad car, pride of Saulito's three-man police force, was parked in front of his home. Inside sat huge Police Chief Pinkerton himself. "Hello, boys!" he boomed as they approached.

"Hello, Chief Pinkerton, your honor, sir," Jerry answered. Only then did he notice something odd about the big policeman. He was minus his usual "G. Barnes, Scientist-Inventor" expression. This was a pleasant surprise.

"Glad to see you, Gerald," the chief rumbled.

Jerry blinked.

"I've been waiting to hear how you captured 'Pig' Nelson."

" 'Pig' Nelson?" Jerry quizzed.

The huge policeman squeezed out of the car. "The motorcycle fellow you tripped up at the fair. Had a record

long as your arm: robbery, grand larceny, unlawful flight
—not to mention attempted murder and arson!"

"Real nice guy, eh?" Jerry quipped.

Chief Pinkerton burst out laughing. He playfully
slapped Jerry on the back. "That's a good one!"

Jerry staggered forward.

"Yes, sir!" the huge man boomed. "Someone telephoned Officer Woods at the station and Woods told me
while I was riding in the opening parade." Chief Pinkerton broke into laughter again. He pounded Jerry's back.
"Yes, sir, Woods came running out with some report about
explosions at the edge of town. When I heard this I asked
myself, 'Now, who would most likely be setting off explosions?' And do you know who I thought of first? G.
Barnes, Scientist-Inventor, that's who!" He raised his
hand to deliver another playful backbreaker, but Jerry
dodged out of reach. "Yes, sir, 'G. Barnes,' I said to myself!"

Jerry nodded. "You can always count on good old G.
Barnes."

"But, of course, it wasn't you at all," the policeman
rumbled, wiping tears of laughter from his eyes. "It was
this Nelson fellow. I picked up his trail. It led right back
to the fairgrounds and you two. This means a lot to the
Saulito Police Department, capturing a nationally known
hoodlum and all." The chief paused to clear his throat. He
took out a little notebook. "I have to make out an official
report to the FBI. Now, then, just how did you capture
him?"

"Who?"

" 'Pig' Nelson . . . the fellow on the motorcycle!' "

"Oh, him! We didn't capture him, your honor, sir. He sort of captured himself. He ran smack-dab into a big ramp. You see, this genius had an underground laboratory where he made the ramp and stored it in a big underground vault under that little shack with the elevator and the TV cameras."

Chief Pinkerton looked puzzled, then burst out laughing. "What a fine sense of humor you have, Gerald!" He delivered another of his tooth-loosening pats. "Underground lab and shacks with elevators! But let's get serious for a moment. This is an official report . . . very important!" He poised his pencil. "Now, just how did you capture this hoodlum?"

Vic stepped forward. "He ran into an invisible ramp, Chief . . ."

". . . that Happy Tom Happy made in an underground laboratory," Jerry added, "filled with all kinds of bottles and tubes and equipment and a five-foot TV screen."

Chief Pinkerton lowered his pencil. The "G. Barnes, Scientist-Inventor" look was beginning to form on his broad face. "All I want to know is how you managed to stop a man riding on a motorcycle," he muttered quietly.

"But Chief Pinkerton, your honor, sir, we told you. It's the truth . . . every word!"

The big man sighed and closed his little notebook. "I'm not asking much . . ." Jerry opened his mouth but the chief waved it shut. "Yes, I know, 'Pig' Nelson ran into

154

an invisible something-or-other which was made in an underground elevator. But how am I going to put that in an official report?" He shook his head sadly and squeezed back into his shiny squad car. "My job would be perfect here in Saulito if it weren't for a very visible *scamp* I keep running into by the name of G. Barnes!"

The squad car shot forward.

CHAPTER 14

Jerry watched Chief Pinkerton drive away. He shrugged. "Looks like we're right back where we started, all-star. Everything has either crumbled, been blown to kingdom come or disappeared. What a deal!"

"Not only that," Vic snorted, "but we're out two bicycles! I'll see you this afternoon, spaceman. Maybe we can at least get a baseball game going."

Sometime later Jerry applied the finishing touches to the rocket model. He backed off from his workbench to admire the gleaming little spaceship. A shower of gravel announced Vic's arrival.

"Let's blast, spaceman. The guys are already down at the park. Hey, that's the greatest!"

"It's a Jupiter X-56," Jerry explained, replacing the

cap on a jar of aluminum paint. "Be with you in a second."

At that moment a shadow slipped across the window. Jerry turned in time to see a dark, heavy-set man step through the open door. Without a word, the man began peering in corners and under tables.

"What . . ." Jerry croaked. "Hey, what are you doing?"

Before he or Vic could make a move, the stranger stepped to the door. "All clear!" he snapped.

Tall, sad-faced Happy Tom Happy appeared.

"Honest Abe!" Jerry blurted. "I mean Happy Tom . . . Mr. Happy!"

The tall man motioned toward the door. "Vic, you'll find something outside that will come in handy for you both."

Vic bolted for the door. He was back in a split second. "Bikes, Jerry! Two brand-new racing bikes! Handle bar brakes, gear shifts and everything!"

Jerry took a step forward, but Mr. Happy held up a bandaged hand. He gestured Vic inside. "I haven't much time. First of all, this is Agent Jackson from the U.S. Security Forces."

"Security?" Jerry reached for his glasses. "Hasn't that got something to do with secrets and spies?"

Happy Tom nodded. "Especially secrets."

"Speaking of secrets, Mr. Happy," Jerry gulped, "I think there's something you ought to know. It's bad news. The presentation was a flop."

"Fine."

Vic broke in. "No, no! Jerry said it was a flop! That

157

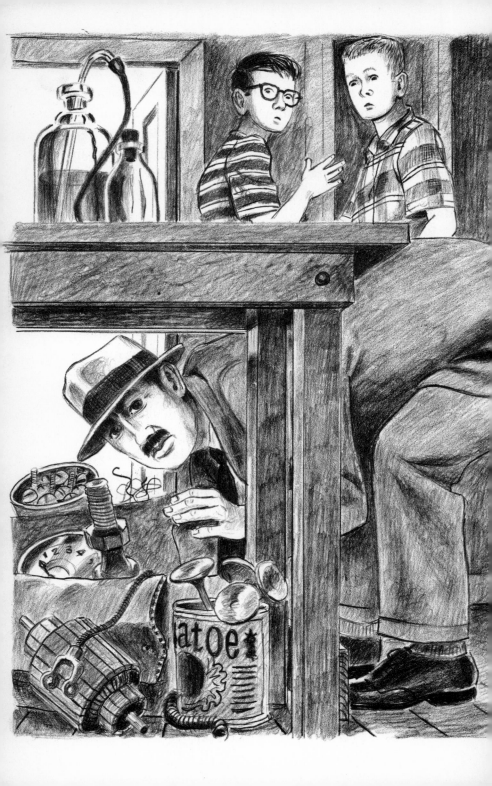

Buck character rammed right into the ramp. We just managed to climb off before the whole thing crumbled to dust. And now nobody in the whole town will believe us . . ."

". . . when you tell them about the invisible ramp," the tall man broke in. "That's just fine."

"But the whole idea was to present transoplastic . . . "

Mr. Happy waved his hand. He signaled and the heavy-set stranger pulled the door shut. "I was in the stand when Buck rammed the ramp."

"In the stand!" Jerry broke in.

"I came back as soon as I had these burns treated. I thought the presentation was a failure, too, until I saw the newspaper photographer take a picture of the three of you scrambling off the crumbling ramp. It took some doing, but I managed to talk the photographer out of the picture."

Jerry fumbled with his glasses. "But I don't see . . ."

Mr. Happy pulled a large Manila envelope from his pocket. He opened it and slipped out a photograph.

Jerry gasped. "That's Mr. Jilliham and Vic . . . and me! Now I remember. When we were crawling down the blocks there was a kind of a flash."

Mr. Happy nodded. "A flying bicycle was spectacular, to say the least, Jerry, but this picture of three people apparently doing a dance in mid-air is even better. With this and the formula I managed to save, I convinced several top government scientists of the value of transoplastic. Thanks to you and Vic, I have been assigned to head a top-secret project."

"Top secret!" Jerry exclaimed.

Happy Tom nodded. "A secret of vital importance to our nation's defense. You'll have to forget everything you've heard or seen. And, most important, you must never mention anything to anyone about Formula T-36."

Vic snorted. "You don't have to worry, Mr. Happy. Nobody believes us, anyway!"

"This is true," the government man murmured. "My reports show that everyone who saw the presentation thinks the bicycle actually flew. This is the best possible thing that could happen. If the subject comes up, you, Barnes, must take all credit."

Jerry blinked.

Mr. Happy stepped forward. "This is probably the last time I'll see you two in quite a while. I'm leaving for Africa tonight."

"Africa!" Jerry exclaimed. "Oh, yes, I remember. One time you told us about the secret sand . . ." He saw the warning frown on the tall scientist's face. "On second thought, I don't remember a thing. How about you, all-star?"

"Huh? Oh, no! Funny—but I can't remember a thing either."

"I want to thank you both for what you've done. Those two bicycles outside can only show part of my apprecia-tion. I will never be able to repay your trust and friend-ship." With that the tall man strode through the door. The government agent followed.

Outside another stranger was busily loading Mr. Happy's gadget-cluttered bicycle into the back of an olive-drab U.S. Army station wagon.

Happy Tom waved as he climbed in. "Hope you enjoy your bikes."

Jerry thought he saw what might have been a smile flash across the man's face, but before he could make sure Happy Tom Happy was out of sight.

Both he and Vic were silent for a moment. Finally Jerry shrugged. "Well, I guess that's that."

Vic stepped closer and glanced around. "I know we're not supposed to talk about it any more, spaceman, but what do you suppose they're going to use that transostuff for?"

"To tell the truth, Vic, I've been trying to figure that myself." He fumbled with his glasses. His glance caught the little rocket ship model gleaming from behind the garage window. "Sure," he whispered.

"Sure what?"

"What could be more important than invisible rocket-launching pads or invisible landing strips for jets . . . or docks for atomic subs . . ."

". . . or backboards for basketball!" Vic added.

"Great galloping galaxies, all-star! Here we are talking about top-secret things and you come up with something like backboards for basketball!"

"Yeah," Vic whispered, "they'll probably make something even more important, like invisible backstops for baseball. Hey, speaking of baseball, let's blast on our brand-new racers, spaceman." He stepped to the gleaming bicycles. "Which one do you want?"

Jerry ran his hand over shiny chrome. "This yellow one, old buddy."

"Good deal! I had my eye on the blue one. Let's try them out by taking a ride . . ."

". . . over to the park where the guys are playing baseball," Jerry interrupted, Happy Tom Happy-like.

"Took the words right out of my mouth, 'Honest Abe.' Let's blast!"

Jimmy Taylor was the first to spot them as they pumped proudly onto the park playground. "Hey, look," he squealed, "it's Jerry and Vic! They have new bikes!"

"Racers," someone else chimed in, "with hand brakes and gear shifts!"

Jerry balanced his bike on the kickstand as the gang gathered around.

"Are thoth flying bithycleth?" pudgy Bob lisped.

"Flying bicycles?"

162

"You know, like you guyth rode in the fair!"

Jerry grinned. "Sounds like one of those crazy inventions G. Barnes might think up."

Bob scratched his head, then he edged closer. "I uth to think your inventionth were crathy, but thath all different now. Thometime when you aren't buthy flying bithycleth or thingth like that, maybe you could find time to fixth up that automatic newthpaper puncher."

Everyone, even the flustered Bob, burst out laughing.

"One thing about G. Barnes," Jimmy Taylor exclaimed, "it doesn't seem to make much difference what anyone says, he keeps right on inventing. And the funniest part, everything seems to work out fine in the end!"

"Right now, let's have a fine game of ball," Vic suggested. "And, spaceman," he added, as they walked out onto the diamond, "try not to let too many easy grounders roll by."

"Sure thing, all-star!" G. Barnes, Scientist-Inventor, answered. Then he jogged toward right field . . . deep right field . . . because his head was already half filled with plans for newer and greater inventions.